NEVER SAY FOREVER

Career girl Kendall McKenzie is determined never to get married. She keeps every man she meets at arm's length . . . and for high-flying businessman Jake Newman, 'no commitment' is his motto. He never lets his heart rule his head. When Kendall and Jake meet they are instantly attracted to each other, but they are both afraid of getting involved. Will their fear of commitment prevent them admitting their love for each other?

KAY HARBORNE

NEVER SAY FOREVER

Complete and Unabridged

LINFORD
Leicester

First published in Great Britain in 2007

First Linford Edition
published 2009

British Library CIP Data

Harborne, Kay.
  Never say forever - -
  (Linford romance library)
  1. Love stories.
  2. Large type books.
  I. Title II. Series
  823.9′2–dc22

  ISBN 978–1–84782–717–3

Published by
F. A. Thorpe (Publishing)
Anstey, Leicestershire

Set by Words & Graphics Ltd.
Anstey, Leicestershire
Printed and bound in Great Britain by
T. J. International Ltd., Padstow, Cornwall

To mum, with love x

An Embarrassing Situation

'Want to go!' yelled Timmy at the top of his voice, stamping his feet.

Kendall sighed. Why had she left it until the last minute to choose an engagement present for Tanya and Hugh? Shopping in a busy department store on a Friday afternoon with a lively three-year-old and a baby in a buggy wasn't what you'd call a relaxing experience. She'd already spent fifteen minutes standing in a queue to pay for the decanter and glasses that she'd chosen, and didn't fancy starting all over again.

'Hang on a minute, Timmy. I'll be served soon and then we'll go and find the toilets, I promise.'

'Now!' Timmy shouted, tugging at her sleeve. 'Want to go now!' he insisted. Then, 'I'll go myself,' he declared. And before Kendall could stop him he turned and ran off.

'Timmy! Come back!' She left the store's wire basket on the floor and, turning baby Sophie's buggy around, set off in hot pursuit of the toddler.

Unfortunately, she hadn't yet mastered the buggy's steering and somehow, instead of going forwards it went sideways . . . slamming into a pair of denim-clad legs.

'Ow!' exclaimed a deep, very masculine voice, and a large, suntanned hand reached down to rub the shin she'd just crashed into.

'Sorry!' She looked up into a pair of gorgeous brown eyes and found herself blushing with embarrassment. Then she remembered Timmy.

She looked around anxiously. Lindsay, his mother, would be horrified if she knew Kendall had taken her eyes off him, even if only for a moment.

'Oh, no!' she gasped as she saw the toddler heading for the escalator that led down to the ground floor. If he stepped on to it and lost his footing . . .

'Timmy! Come back!' she yelled,

trying to run after him, but was hindered by the cumbersome buggy.

'It's OK. I'll get him.' The owner of the bruised shin and the gorgeous brown eyes was already sprinting across the shop, his impressive height and long legs making it easy for him to dodge through the crowds.

Kendall bit her lip as she followed him, pushing the buggy as quickly as she could and praying that he would reach Timmy — who was by now dangerously near the top of the escalator — in time.

People turned their heads to look, obviously wondering what was going on.

As the toddler reached the escalator and put out a foot to step on to it, Kendall felt a cold shiver of fear run down her spine; then, as he was scooped up just in time by the handsome stranger, she let out a sigh of relief.

'Come on, young man, your mummy wants you. That escalator's too dangerous for you to go on by yourself.'

Timmy was staring wide-eyed at his rescuer as he was carried back to Kendall, who had finally managed to battle her way through the crowds.

'It was really naughty to run off like that,' she scolded. 'Don't you ever do that again!'

She reached out as the man handed the child over to her. Their hands touched briefly and she felt a tingle run up her arm. Feeling her cheeks flush yet again, she was grateful for the chance to hide her face as she bent over to put Timmy down.

'Now, hold on to the buggy and stay by me,' she ordered.

'Want a wee-wee!' Timmy told her urgently, screwing up his face.

'I think perhaps you'd better take him to the loo before he makes a puddle on the floor,' said the man. 'The toilets are over there. Will I look after the baby while you take him? You'd be quicker if you didn't have to take that pushchair with you.'

She couldn't leave baby Sophie with

a complete stranger! Even a very friendly, handsome stranger who had just saved Timmy from a dreadful accident. What would Lindsay say?

'Look, I'm not going to kidnap the baby if that's what you're worrying about.' The man took his wallet out of his pocket and handed her a credit card. 'Here, I'll trust you with my credit card if you'll trust me with your baby. And for goodness sake get a move on! I don't think your little boy can wait any longer.'

One look at Timmy told her that the man was right.

'OK. Thanks.' She took the credit card from him, grabbed the toddler's hand, and hurried to the ladies' toilets.

'I can do it myself!' Timmy told her firmly.

'You can? Fine. I'll wait for you out here. But don't lock the door — OK?' And she waited for him by the entrance to the loos, positioning herself so that she could keep watch on both Timmy and his little sister, who seemed quite unperturbed about being left in the care of . . . Jake Newman was the name on the gold card.

Well, Jake Newman wasn't short of a penny or two — this was a very exclusive credit card only granted to the mega-rich. Rich and handsome, she thought. Quite a catch for someone.

Not her though. She wasn't interested in catching anyone. No commitment was her motto. There was no way she was going to have her heart broken by a man. She'd seen it happen to her friends too often. Just look at how Lindsay had been treated by her ex-husband, Adam.

Everyone had thought that Adam and Lindsay would be together forever, but he'd walked out on her just three years after their wedding, to set up home with a PR girl named Alixia, leaving a pregnant, devastated Lindsay to pick up the pieces of her life and to bring up Timmy by herself.

She'd got over his betrayal eventually, finding love with her second husband, Matt, and going on to have baby

Sophie. But Kendall had vowed that she would never let anyone have the power to hurt her the way that Adam had hurt her best friend. How did the saying go; the one who loved the most got hurt the most? Well, she was determined that she would never love anyone enough to get hurt. She had a good job and a hectic social life with a group of close friends. She didn't need a man in her life. She had boyfriends, yes, but was always careful never to let her relationships get serious.

'What's that?'

Timmy's voice brought her out of her daydream.

'It's a credit card and it belongs to that nice man who saved you from tumbling down the escalator,' she told him. 'Now wash your hands and let's go get Sophie.'

'I've already washed them,' he told her.

Had he? How long had she been standing there, deep in thought?

'Come on, then.' She grabbed his

hand and led him out into the store, to where Jake Newman was playing peek-a-boo with Sophie.

The baby chuckled as he moved behind the back of the buggy so that she couldn't see him, then popped his head out — 'Boo!'

Timmy laughed and Jake quickly stood up, grinning ruefully.

'I thought I'd better try to amuse her,' he told Kendall.

'Thank you. And thank you again for rescuing Timmy.' She smiled at him as she handed back his credit card.

As he took it from her, his fingers brushed against hers and she felt that tingle shoot up her arm again and, as his eyes met hers, she felt herself drowning in their deep, brown pools. This guy really was something she thought, pulling herself together as she realised he was talking to her.

'Sorry . . . mm . . . what did you say?'

'I said that maybe you should leave the kids at home with your husband next time you go shopping. It would

8

make things easier for you.'

'I haven't got a husband. I'm not married. I mean — '

'Look, you don't have to explain your life story to me,' he said, a slight edge to his voice. 'Now, if you'll excuse me I've got some shopping of my own to do.'

'Yes, of course. Thank you again . . . ' But he was already walking away.

She watched for a moment as he made his way through the crowds, noticing the way that his thick dark hair curled at the nape of his neck.

She thought of those dreamy brown eyes . . . then she shook her head, wondering how he could have had such an effect on her when they'd only spoken for a few minutes.

It was just as well she'd be unlikely to bump into him again — with or without the buggy. She had an idea that, if she'd had the chance to get to know him better, this guy wouldn't be easy to forget — and her plans for the future didn't include pining over some bloke.

'Auntie Kendy, can we go home

now?' Timmy tugged at her sleeve and she pulled herself together, suddenly remembering the crystal decanter set that she'd left in the basket at the till.

'Just a few more minutes, Timbo,' she promised, using her pet name for him. 'I've got to go back to pay for something, then we can go.'

She hoped that the basket containing the present she'd chosen for Tanya and Hugh was still there but, thankfully, the lady at the till had kept it behind the counter, guessing she'd go back for it once she'd taken Timmy to the toilet.

She gratefully paid for her purchases and headed for the lift.

Glancing at her watch she saw that it was almost time for Sophie's feed and knew that Lindsay would be anxiously waiting for them. Whilst her friend loved a break from the children, she could never completely relax when they were out of her sight, even though she knew they were safe with Kendall.

Safe! That was a joke! If Lindsay knew about Timmy's narrow escape she'd have a fit and probably refuse to let her take the children out again. She decided not to mention it. No need to upset her friend unnecessarily.

★ ★ ★

So much for keeping Timmy's escapade quiet! He told his mum all about his adventure as soon as they got through the door.

'I was going for a wee-wee and got lost,' he babbled. 'Then a nice man picked me up and took me back to Auntie Kendy.'

'What?' Lindsay shot Kendall a worried look as she took Timmy in her arms.

'It wasn't as bad as it sounds,' Kendall assured her, quickly explaining.

'You mean that Timmy was about to step on to the escalator? That high escalator that runs all the way down to the ground floor?' Lindsay's voice was almost a squeak.

'I'm sorry, he just ran off. But it's

OK. Jake got to him in time.'

'Jake? I thought you didn't know this man?'

Kendall sighed. Now she had to explain about swopping baby Sophie for Jake Newman's credit card while she took Timmy to the loo, and what would Lindsay make of that?

When she'd finished, her friend looked at her knowingly.

'And what exactly was this man like?' she asked.

A picture flashed into Kendall's mind: twinkling eyes the colour of treacle fudge; thick, dark, slightly curly hair; a definitely good-looking face; tall, lean body . . .

'That good, eh?' Lindsay was watching her with amusement.

Kendall tried to sound casual. 'He was OK,' she admitted.

'So, will you be seeing each other again?'

'Hardly!' Kendall laughed. 'We didn't exchange phone numbers or anything. I really have to dash now, Lindsay. I've got to get ready for Tanya and Hugh's party tonight.'

'Just stay for coffee and you can show me the pressie you bought and fill me in on what you're going to wear,' Lindsay begged.

'OK, just a quick coffee,' she agreed.

★   ★   ★

It was almost six o'clock by the time she returned home to her flat. That meant she had just over an hour and a half to fix herself something to eat, and to have a shower and get changed before Emma and the taxi arrived. Emma only lived a few minutes drive away, so it made sense to share a taxi to the party.

By the time she'd made and eaten a cheese omelette it was almost half-past six. Less than an hour left to get ready! No time to put her hair up; she'd have to leave it loose.

Thankfully, she'd already decided on what she was going to wear — the emerald-green silk dress she'd bought last Christmas. The colour matched her eyes and complimented her rich-brown hair, whilst the simple cut showed off her slim figure.

'You'll wow everyone in that dress,' Lindsay had said approvingly when Kendall had told her what she was planning to wear. 'I bet you end up with a date. Phone me tomorrow and tell me all about it.'

'There'll be nothing to tell,' Kendall had replied. 'It's an engagement party. There'll only be Tanya and Hugh's family and friends there.'

'Yes, but Hugh's bound to have some cute friends,' Lindsay had teased.

Not as cute as Jake Newman. The thought had startled Kendall. What was wrong with her? Had it been so long since she'd had a boyfriend that she fantasised over every man she met now? If that was the case, then maybe Lindsay was right and it was time she had a bit of light-hearted romance in her life.

The downstairs buzzer sounded just as she'd finished applying her lipstick. She glanced at the clock. It was half-past seven; the taxi — and Emma — were bang on time.

'Are you ready, Kendy?' Emma's voice came over the intercom.

Kendall stood up and surveyed her reflection in the mirror. She'd decided to wear her latest jewellery designs — a jade pendant and matching earrings — which complimented her dress perfectly. She'd made a really unusual silver clasp and chain from which to hang the pendant and was pleased with the effect.

'I'm on my way!' she called into the intercom, grabbing her bag and the now wrapped engagement present as she headed for the door.

* * *

Tanya and Hugh had hired a room at a local hotel for their engagement party.

It was a good choice, Kendall thought, as she and Emma walked in. It was a smallish room with a cosy, friendly atmosphere. There was a cold buffet laid out and an up-and-coming local band were setting up their instruments by the far wall where space had been cleared for people to dance. Quite a lot of guests had already arrived and were chatting away to each other.

'Very nice,' Emma said, looking around. 'Hey, isn't that Pete Taylor over there?'

'Pete Taylor?' Kendall frowned as she tried to recall who he was.

'You remember, the good-looking blond kid who everyone fancied at school? He's over at the bar.'

Kendall looked across to see a handsome blond-haired man looking back at them. Yes, she remembered Pete, and from the way he was waving, he remembered them, too. He picked up his drink and walked over.

'Emma Claxton and Kendall Mc-Kenzie.' He smiled. 'Well, you two look even more gorgeous than you did at school.'

'Why, thank you, kind sir.' Emma grinned, bobbing a mock curtsy. 'And you're looking quite nice yourself. Isn't he, Kendy?'

'Hmm.' Kendall pretended to study Pete, a critical expression on her face. 'Your hair's a big improvement, that's for sure.'

They all laughed. Pete had been in trouble at school on more than one occasion because his hair was too long.

* * *

Jake had been watching her from the moment she'd walked into the room. Now she was deep in conversation with a smooth-looking blond man and a vivacious-looking dark-haired girl. The man must be her boyfriend, he thought.

She looked so heart-stoppingly beautiful in an emerald dress that fitted her perfectly, accentuating her figure. Her wavy, warm-brown hair cascaded over her shoulders and he longed to run his fingers through it. A delicate jade necklace hung around her neck on an intricate silver chain and, when she flung back her head as she laughed at something the blond guy was saying, Jake saw that she was wearing matching jade earrings.

Then her boyfriend touched her on the arm and she nodded as he walked off to the bar, while she and her dark-haired friend headed across the room towards Tanya and Hugh.

Jake felt his mouth go dry as he watched her walk away. He felt an overpowering urge to talk to her again and to find out more about her.

Stay away, he told himself, she's got two children and a partner.

So why did he find himself following in her footsteps?

Kendall felt the hair on the back of her neck rise as her body sensed someone approaching her from behind — someone that made her senses tingle. She turned around and was astonished when she saw who was walking towards her. She stared at him, hardly able to believe her eyes.

For goodness sake, close your mouth and pull yourself together, she told herself; you must look like a demented goldfish!

Emma followed her gaze and whistled appreciatively.

'Who is that?'

'Jake Newman, a friend of Hugh's from his university days,' Tanya told her. 'He's a real hunk, isn't he?'

'Hey, you're not supposed to be looking at other men at our engagement party,' Hugh teased.

'Don't be silly, darling, you know I've only got eyes for you,' Tanya told him, pecking him on the cheek.

'Haven't you two got tired of each other yet?' Jake quipped as he joined the group.

Tanya turned to smile at him. 'Glad you could make it, Jake.'

'I wouldn't have missed it for the world,' he said. 'I can't believe you've managed to ensnare him at last! You're letting the side down, Hugh.'

'Your turn will come,' Hugh told him. 'You can't fight it forever, mate.'

'Never!' Jake grinned. Then he turned to Kendall. 'Hello, again.'

Tanya looked surprised. 'Do you two know each other?' she asked.

'We met briefly this afternoon,' Kendall explained, trying to keep the wobble out of her voice. He looked even more handsome than she remembered.

'But we didn't get around to introductions,' he said. 'We were a bit too busy with the children.'

'Children?' Tanya raised an enquiring eyebrow.

'I took Lindsay's kids shopping, to give her a break,' Kendall explained, for Jake's benefit as much as Tanya's. 'Timmy ran off and was about to step on to the escalator when Jake came to my rescue.'

'A knight in shining armour, eh?' said Emma, looking at Jake admiringly.

'I wish I had been wearing armour. Then I wouldn't have a whopping great bruise on my shin!' he replied, his eyes twinkling.

Kendall looked guilty. 'I am sorry about that. I was in such a rush to chase after Timmy that I rammed the buggy into Jake's legs,' she explained to the others. 'Honestly, I don't know how Lindsay manages to manoeuvre it, it's really awkward.'

'Maybe she's had more practice than you,' Jake suggested. 'I take it that you don't often take your friend's children shopping?'

'Actually, I often help Lindsay with her kids when I'm in this country but I don't usually lose them.'

'In this country? Do you live abroad then?'

'Kendall travels the world teaching English as a foreign language,' Tanya told him. 'She's just come back from Spain, haven't you, Kendy?'

'Really? How interesting.' His eyes held hers. 'And how many different countries have you worked in?'

'Hmm, let me see ... China, Australia, France, Thailand and, of course, Spain — which is where my parents live nowadays,' she told him. 'One of the advantages of being footloose and fancy-free is that you can up sticks and go off whenever the fancy takes you.'

'I keep telling her that she'll meet the right man some day and settle down,' added Tanya. 'But she's as bad as you, Jake. Determined to stay unattached.'

'And will you be in England for a while or is this just a fleeting visit?' he asked her.

'I've no firm plans as yet. I'll get some temping work in an office to tide me over for a while before I decide which part of the world I'd like to see next.'

'Your drinks, ladies.' Pete joined them, handing first Kendall, then Emma, a glass of white wine. 'What's this about going abroad again?'

Jake's mind was racing. So she has no

commitments at the moment, he thought, but if Pete had anything to do with it she soon would have, and he wondered why that knowledge bothered him.

'So you're looking for temporary work?' he asked. 'Well, I'm looking for a temporary secretary because mine has just broken her ankle. Do you fancy taking over her job for a few weeks until she's fit enough to return?'

The words were out before he knew what he was saying.

'Are you serious?' Kendall turned to look at him, her green eyes wide with surprise.

'Absolutely. As I said, it'll only be for a few weeks. You'd be working at my new offices in Birmingham city centre. Answering the phone, dealing with customers, etc. Think you could handle it?'

'Go on, Kendy; you need a job,' Tanya urged. 'And Jake needs a secretary. It's an ideal solution.'

He could see that she was swithering

and he realised that for some reason he couldn't fathom — he'd hardly said more than a dozen words to the woman, for goodness' sake — he desperately wanted her to take the job.

'I'd need you to start on Monday. What do you say?'

Kendall tilted her chin and looked him straight in the eye. She saw a challenge there and something else, too. Something dangerous. A thrilling current moved through her as he held her gaze. His nearness both disturbed and excited her. All her senses responded to this man.

Her heart screamed at her to take the job so that she could be near him but her mind was telling her to keep her distance. Don't be stupid, she told herself, you need a job and he's offering you one. You'd be a fool to turn it down. So what if you do find him attractive? That's not to say he's attracted to you.

But he was. She could feel it. The mutual attraction was crackling in the air between them.

'OK,' she heard herself say. 'So you'd want me to start this Monday?'

'That's right.' He handed her a card. 'There's the address. If you could be there just before nine?'

She took the card and looked at it. *EXA Electronics.* She'd heard of the company. It was a well-known international computer software firm. And the address was that of one of the posh new office blocks on the outskirts of the city centre, near to the International Conference Centre and the National Indoor Arena. Very impressive.

'No problem,' she told him. 'I'll be there.'

A New Job

'Well, how did the party go?' Lindsay asked eagerly, the following day. She'd left the children with Matt and popped in to see Kendall to catch up on all the gossip. 'Did you meet anyone interesting?'

A picture of Jake Newman flickered into Kendall's mind. She sipped her coffee slowly and tried to look casual.

'There were lots of interesting people there,' she replied. 'It was a really good evening.'

'You met a man, didn't you?' Lindsay squealed in delight. 'Don't bother to deny it. I can tell by that dreamy look in your eyes. Who is he? Have you got a date?'

'No, but I have got a job.'

'A job? That's brilliant! Now you might stay in England for a while and we can see more of each other! What sort of job is it? And how did you get it?'

'I'm going to be a temporary secretary at a computer software firm in town. Someone offered me the job at the party last night.'

Lindsay scrutinised her suspiciously. 'Why do I get the feeling you're keeping something from me?'

'Do you want biscuits with your coffee?' Kendall asked, hoping to distract her friend while she found the words to explain how it was Jake Newman who had offered her the job, without giving away the fact that even thinking about him made her pulse race.

'Chocolate digestives or bourbon creams, or both?' she asked, getting up to fetch the biscuit tin.

'Both, please. Now, sit down and tell me about what you'll be doing.'

'I told you, I'm to be a secretary for a computer software firm.'

'But who offered you the job?' Lindsay bit into a chocolate digestive.

'Honestly, Lindsay, you're so suspicious. It's no big deal. A friend of Hugh's needs a secretary because his PA has broken her ankle. He heard I was looking for a job and that was that.'

'And who exactly is this friend?' Lindsay mumbled, still nibbling her biscuit.

'Someone Hugh went to university with.'

'Kendy, I know there's something you're not telling me.'

'Well, if you must know, it's Jake Newman. You know, the guy I met when I was shopping? The one who saved Timmy from the escalator?'

'The one you fancy like mad?' Lindsay added, a smug smile on her face.

'I do not so!' retorted Kendall.

'Oh, come on, you've gone all dewy-eyed.'

'OK, so I admit he's good-looking and some people might fancy him.'

Some people! Who was she trying to kid; any red-blooded female would find him attractive.

'But he's not my type. He offered me

the job because he needs a secretary and I accepted because I need a job. End of story.'

'Then why are you being so coy about it?'

'Because I know you'll try to make something of it, that's why! You're always trying to matchmake, hoping I'll fall in love and live happily ever after. And I keep telling you — I don't believe in that rubbish. I'm happy being single.'

Lindsay's face softened and she reached across to place her hand on Kendall's. 'Don't let what happened between myself and Adam make you hard and bitter,' she said quietly. 'He hurt me badly but it was a long time ago. I've moved on and found happiness again with Matt. I'd like you to find someone to love, too.'

'I'm pleased for you, Lindsay, but I'm not like you,' Kendall told her. 'I don't need a man to make me happy. I like my life just as it is. I'm free to come and go as I please. I don't want to be tied down.'

'Being in love isn't about being tied down. It's about caring for each other, sharing things and having someone to lean on.'

'I don't want someone to share my life with or to lean on,' Kendall quipped. 'Miss Independent, that's me. Now how about another coffee?'

★ ★ ★

Jake couldn't stop thinking about her all weekend; the way her emerald-green eyes twinkled when she laughed, how she kept flicking back her luscious cascade of rich-brown hair, the fullness of her lips, the creamy white of her skin.

Her name suited her, he thought. Kendall. It suggested someone unusual, exotic, a free spirit. And he wanted to get to know her better, yet the thought made him feel . . . afraid somehow. Something about her got right under his skin. Well, he'd have to make sure he kept things completely platonic between them.

If there was one thing he didn't believe in, it was mixing business with pleasure.

So why had he asked her to work for him? So that he could see her again, be near her, but couldn't get involved with her? Why put himself through that? He shook the disturbing thoughts from his mind. He needed a secretary and she needed a job. That was all there was to it.

* * *

Kendall left home at just after eight o'clock on Monday morning, to allow plenty of time for any hold-ups with the traffic. She wanted to make sure she arrived early on her first day in her new job.

She pressed the remote control to unlock the doors of the ancient red Fiesta that she used as a runabout whenever she returned to England. She rented out her flat while she worked abroad and, although the wages from teaching English as a foreign language weren't very high, she usually got free or cheap board thrown in, which meant she had modest savings.

She didn't intend to waste her money on a flash car though. She'd always dreamed of setting up her own jewellery design business and, one day, when she'd saved enough, that's exactly what she was going to do.

She opened the car door, slid into the driving seat and turned on the ignition. At least while she was driving she'd have to keep her mind on the road instead of letting it drift towards Jake Newman, as it had done for most of the weekend.

★　★　★

Standing in front of a class of foreign students, in the many different countries she'd worked in, had soon taught Kendall to keep her nerves under control. Now, she hardly felt nervous at all when she started a new job.

So why were butterflies doing somersaults in her stomach today?

Because you're nervous about seeing Jake again, a niggling little voice told her.

She'd heard that the new office blocks in the city centre were impressive but hadn't realised *how* impressive, and she took a deep breath as she approached EXA Electronics' modern, cylindrical building, with its white pillars at the front entrance and walls of tinted glass that towered up to the sky.

She wondered how many floors there were, then the automatic front doors opened and she stepped into the foyer and looked around. The thick, blue carpet shouted luxury, as did the expensive oil paintings, ultra modern sculptures and exotic, tropical plants that were scattered about, seemingly casually arranged but obviously strategically placed for maximum effect. And just in case there was any doubt about how important the company was, uniformed security guards were placed by the entrance.

An attractive, well-groomed, middle-aged woman was standing behind the large reception desk, tapping at the keys of a computer. She looked up as Kendall approached.

'You must be Kendall McKenzie, Mr Newman's temporary secretary,' she said, with a welcoming smile. 'I'm Sylvia Cartier. Mr Newman asked me to greet you and direct you to his office. He's on the sixth floor, right at the end of the corridor. You can't miss his room, his name is on the door.'

'Thank you.' Kendall smiled back. The woman's friendly manner put her at ease. 'Has he arrived yet?'

'Oh, yes, Mr Newman is always here early.' The receptionist keyed something into the computer then looked up again. 'It's such a shame about Joyce breaking her ankle. Mr Newman relies on her so much. She's very efficient. I'm afraid you're going to have your work cut out doing her job.'

'I'll do my best. The sixth floor you said?'

'That's right. The lifts are over there, to your left.'

'Thank you.' Kendall walked over to the three lifts, positioned side by side along the wall. There were several people waiting for them — all, like the receptionist, well-groomed and smartly dressed. Her first impressions of this company were very good, she acknowledged — glad she'd decided to wear her smart, grey suit and had put her hair up. At least she looked like a professional secretary even if her tummy was full of collywobbles.

But it wasn't starting a new job that was making her nervous, she acknowledged. It was the thought of meeting Jake Newman again.

Don't be daft, she told herself. You're acting like a schoolgirl with a crush.

She had no problem finding his office. As the receptionist had told her, the words *Jake Newman, Director*, were engraved on a gold plate on the door.

He was obviously a man of importance. Then she smiled as she remembered how she'd rammed Sophie's buggy into this important man's legs on Friday.

She squared her shoulders, knocked firmly on the door and stepped inside.

Jake was sitting, leaning back, in a black leather chair, talking on the phone. He looked every inch the powerful business man today, devastatingly handsome in his dark suit, immaculate, white shirt and midnight-blue tie. He smiled at her, indicating that she should come in and take a seat, then continued with his phone conversation.

She sank into a soft leather sofa and looked around. It was an impressive office — modern and relaxing — furnished with a mahogany desk and cupboards, and several matching leather chairs as well as the sofa. A selection of glossy magazines was piled neatly on a long, low table and, she noticed, in a corner of the room there was a state-of-the-art coffee machine, together with several china cups and saucers.

A large window took up most of one

of the walls of the room, allowing her to see through into the office next door, where most of the floor space was taken up by an enormous ebony desk and director's chair.

So *that* was Jake's office, she realised, and *this* office must be hers. The leather sofa was where visitors waited for Jake to summon them into his inner sanctum, whilst she served them coffee, no doubt.

'Sorry about that,' he said, replacing the receiver. He rose from his seat and held out a hand. 'Welcome to EXA Electronics.'

She rose too, and as his hand clasped hers she felt her senses tingle yet again. She knew he felt the same way. She could tell by the way his hand lingered over hers and his eyes darkened.

'What would you like me to do first?' she asked, struggling to keep her voice under control.

'Please, sit down and I'll go through your duties with you. You've already guessed that this is your office while I usually work through there?' He jerked a thumb towards the open door behind him.

'Yes, I figured the posh desk would be yours,' she teased. 'But I don't mind trading it for the coffee machine.'

Something flickered across his face. Annoyance perhaps at her flippant tone? She really ought to act in a more businesslike manner, she chided herself. After all, she didn't really know Jake. Not enough to act so familiarly with him.

'That's clever planning,' he told her, with a smile. 'We get to share the coffee but you're the one who has to make it.'

So she hadn't annoyed him, she thought with relief.

'Now, I'd better run though a few things with you,' he told her.

She listened attentively as he explained her various duties, handing her an audio-tape containing letters he'd dictated for her to type up, and a card with his personal mobile number.

'You're familiar with a computer?' he asked. 'And the filing system should be self-explanatory. Joyce is very efficient.'

'No problem,' she told him.

'Good. Oh, and you need to fill in your details on this form for personnel. I have to go out now. I've an important meeting to attend.' He walked around the desk towards her. 'I might be gone all morning. Do you think you can manage?'

'Of course,' she said briskly. 'Do you want me to contact you if anything urgent crops up or shall I wait until you get back?'

'Please don't contact me unless it's an absolute emergency. The meeting is with a valued client and I don't want to be disturbed.'

He was standing in front of her now, towering above her, and she stood up to put herself on an equal footing but realised immediately that she'd made a mistake. She was too close to him. Their bodies were mere centimetres apart and hers was screaming to get closer, to touch him. She quickly stepped past him and walked around the desk to the chair he'd just vacated.

'Well, I guess I'd better make a start,' she said, sitting down in the chair which was still warm from his body. Another big mistake. Just the knowledge that she was sitting in the very place where he'd just been, was unsettling. What was the matter with her? Anyone would think she'd never met an attractive man before.

She felt his eyes upon her and she forced herself to meet his gaze, pasting a bright smile on her face. 'I'll see you later, then,' she said confidently.

She switched on the computer and turned her attention to the flickering screen, hoping that she was giving the impression of a professional secretary intent on doing her job well.

She heard him walk across the room and hesitate in the doorway, but she kept her gaze on the computer screen until she heard a click as the door closed behind him.

She let out a deep breath and looked up. What was it about this guy that affected her so much? It was as if every nerve in her body responded to him to the extent that just being in the same building as him was electrifying. His very presence seemed to fill and dominate the room. Throw in good looks and a lean body and you had an irresistible combination, she acknowledged ruefully.

The shrill ringing of the telephone startled her and she automatically picked up the receiver. 'Good morning. This is Mr Newman's office. Can I help you?'

'Good morning! You must be Kendall,' a friendly voice replied. 'I'm Joyce, Jake's secretary. I thought I'd phone to see how you were getting on.'

'That's very kind of you, Joyce. How are you feeling? Is your ankle any better?' Kendall asked, thinking how nice it was of the woman to phone her like this.

'Oh, it's fine providing I don't walk on it, so I'm sitting here bored out of my mind — hence this phone call. I presume you're from Pronto Temps?'

'No, actually I met Jake — Mr Newman — on Friday evening, at a mutual friend's engagement party.' She explained briefly how she'd just arrived back in the UK and how Jake had offered her a job. 'He's gone out to a meeting so I was just about to acquaint myself with the filing system.'

'Yes, he's got an early meeting with Clive Dorking, of CD Computer Systems. I'd better fill you in about that, then I'll tell you who's who so you know who to put through immediately if they call and who to tell that Jake will phone them back. After that, I'll explain the filing system. It's pretty straightforward so you should soon master it.'

'That would be wonderful. Thank you.' Kendall picked up a pen and began to make notes as Joyce talked.

★ ★ ★

Jake wasn't normally one to let his attention stray in the middle of a business meeting. For him work came first, second and third. None of his many beautiful women friends had ever encroached upon his thoughts when he was working. So why then did he keep thinking about a girl he hardly knew? Try as he might to push her away, Kendall McKenzie wouldn't leave his mind. Her face, her perfume, the way she walked . . . things he hadn't even known he'd noticed about her were locked away in his memory and flashes of them kept slipping through. The way she smiled, the sound of her voice . . .

'So what do you think, Jake? Is it a deal?'

Darn! What on earth had Clive been talking about? Jake's normally razorsharp mind played back the conversation. They'd been talking about the terms of the deal but he couldn't recall what Clive had actually suggested.

'Well, it sounds good . . . ' he said slowly, as if he was giving it some consideration, all the time playing for time, hoping that Clive would give him a clue as to what he'd been saying.

'Good? I'll say it's good! You'll have the majority share of the business. I'll just be taking a back seat and leaving you to it. And it's the lowest price I'll accept. You won't beat me down.'

He mentioned a figure that Jake knew was more than fair.

'OK.' He nodded. 'You've got a deal — subject to my lawyers giving it the once over, of course.'

He stood up and held out his hand.

Clive's face flooded with relief. CD Computer Systems was in trouble, but he knew Jake could save it and he'd guaranteed jobs for all his staff.

'Good to do business with you, Jake.' They shook hands firmly. 'I'll get my solicitors to draft the papers right away. They'll be with you by the end of the week.'

★   ★   ★

Thank goodness for Joyce's phone call, Kendall thought as she finished typing

44

the letters Jake had dictated. She'd never have been able to find the Jenson file without her help. As it was, she'd now been able to type up the quote and everything was ready for Jake to sign when he came back.

She glanced at her watch. It was almost lunch time and he'd been gone all morning. It must have been a very important appointment.

The phone rang again and she reached out to take the call, her eyes flicking towards the list of 'Important People' that Joyce had dictated to her.

'Hi, Kendall,' a male voice drawled and her mind did a double-take as she tried to think who it could be. 'It's Pete. I wondered if we could meet for lunch. There's something I wanted to talk to you about.'

Of course, Pete Taylor! He'd heard Jake offer her the job at the party — although he'd have had to do a bit of detective work to find the name of the firm and the number for Jake's office. Mind you, it didn't take two guesses to figure out who had told him — Tanya. But she was pleased he'd called. It would be nice to have lunch with a friend on her first day.

'That would be lovely, Pete,' she said, just as the office door opened and Jake stepped in. 'What time shall we meet and where?'

She saw Jake's eyes darken and his shoulders stiffen, and she realised how it must look to him, returning from an important meeting to find her taking personal calls on her very first morning.

'Yes, that will be fine. I'll meet you there,' she said quickly. 'I've got to go now. I'm really busy.' She put down the receiver and looked at Jake who was now standing rather impatiently by her desk. 'Sorry about that. It was Pete — remember you met him on Friday night? Tanya must have given him your number.'

'How kind of her.'

Kendall was surprised at the sarcasm in his voice.

'Sorry, I promise not to make a habit

of taking personal calls at work — and I did keep it brief. It's just that Pete . . . '

'Don't worry about it,' he cut in dismissively. 'Now, is there anything that needs my attention before I go to lunch myself?'

'I've typed those letters for you.' She indicated the pile of correspondence waiting in the out tray on her desk. 'And I took the liberty of typing up the Jenson quote. Joyce phoned and told me where the file was. She gave me quite a lot of useful information, so I've made a few notes.'

Pull yourself together, Kendall, you're gabbling, she told herself. But something about the way he was looking at her made her knees quiver.

'And how is Joyce?' he asked, picking up the letters.

'She's fine, but bored,' she told him, trying to keep her voice steady. If only he wasn't standing quite so close to her. She was sure he could hear her heart pounding in her chest. 'She said she can't wait to come back to work.'

'I can imagine. Joyce likes to be kept busy.' He flashed her a dazzling smile.

He sure changes moods fast, she thought.

'Arrange for flowers to be sent to her, will you? They might cheer her up a bit. Enclose a note with them, wishing her well. And how did your first morning go? No problems I hope?'

'None I couldn't handle. Thanks to Joyce.'

Then her heart turned over as his eyes met hers. The silence stretched taut between them, the air tingling with anticipation as his face came closer. Mesmerised, she raised her lips to meet his.

Then the door was flung open. 'Jake, darling, I'm back!'

She heard his sharp intake of breath, saw something flash in his eyes, then his face was composed as he stepped away from her, picking up the letters from the desk as he did so.

'I'll sign these now, Kendall,' he said. Then he turned towards the door.

'Hello, Leticia. I hope you had a good trip?'

Kendall followed his gaze towards the beautiful blonde standing in the doorway. Tall, slim, and elegantly dressed in clothes that shouted designer, the girl stared coolly back at her.

'I see you've got a new secretary? What's happened to Joyce?'

'She's broken her ankle. Miss McKenzie is filling in for her.'

'Is she now?' Leticia raised a well-groomed eyebrow. 'You're very young, aren't you, dear?' she remarked. 'Are you sure you've got enough experience to handle this job?'

Kendall knew immediately that the other woman looked on her as a threat.

'I'll do my best,' she said serenely. She turned to Jake. 'It is all right if I take my lunch now, Mr Newman?'

'Yes, of course. You don't want to be late for your date,' he replied curtly.

Leticia smiled at this remark. 'Boyfriend, is it?'

'Just a friend,' Kendall told her,

picking up her bag. 'Nice to meet you, Miss Sinclair.'

She walked out of the office, pleased at the look of surprise on Leticia's face when she'd used her surname. According to Joyce, Jake and Leticia had been an item for a while, but Jake had grown tired of her possessiveness and had been trying to break-off the relationship — Leticia, however, wouldn't let him go.

She looked the sort of woman who wouldn't let anything stand between her and her man, Kendall thought as she walked over to the lift and pressed the button. She'd made that quite clear.

Jake was hers. Hands off.

Not that she needed to issue any warnings to Kendall. Kendall had no intention of getting involved with Jake Newman. None at all.

Then why had she been about to let him kiss her before Leticia had walked in?

A Business Trip

You idiot! Kendall told herself as she made her way to the pub where she'd arranged to meet Pete. It was only a few minutes walk so she'd left her car behind, hoping the fresh air would clear her head. She couldn't believe that she had actually been about to kiss Jake Newman! She'd only been working for him for a few hours and already she was throwing herself at her boss. But he'd made the first move, she reminded herself, and nothing had actually happened. Only by sheer luck, she grudgingly admitted. She'd been quite ready and willing to melt into his arms. What had got into her?

OK, she fancied him like mad but that was no excuse. She'd met his type before — and they were all predators. All good looks and smooth talk. Men like him charmed you off your feet, then next thing you're nursing a broken heart and they've moved on to their next conquest.

Well, she had no intention of becoming one of Jake Newman's cast-offs. Or anyone else's for that matter.

From now on she was going to keep herself firmly under control and well out of his clutches. She would be polite, but formal and businesslike.

★ ★ ★

'Hiya, Kendy.' Pete was seated at a table near the door, waiting for her. 'How's the new job?'

'Fine,' she told him, sitting down beside him. 'Though I don't think my boss was too impressed by you phoning me on my first day.'

'Sorry about that.' He grinned ruefully. 'Aren't you allowed personal calls?'

'I'm sure the occasional one is fine but I could have done without any this morning. Never mind, you weren't to know. Now, what was so important that you had to see me today?'

'Shall we order, first?' Pete suggested. 'What do you fancy? My treat.'

She picked up the menu and quickly scanned it. 'I'll just have a ham salad, please. And a mineral water. I don't like a heavy lunch.'

'I do, I'm starving.' Pete went up to the bar and ordered salad for Kendall and steak pie, chips and a pint of lager for himself.

'Emma told me you designed and made the necklace you were wearing at the party on Friday night,' he said, as he sat back down. 'She said you design lots of jewellery.'

'That's right. It's a hobby at the moment, but I'm hoping to develop it into a career, eventually.'

'Well, it's my mum's birthday next month. She'll be fifty and I need to find a special gift for her.' He took a long sip of his lager before continuing. 'I was wondering if you would make something for her? A brooch perhaps, or a bracelet?'

'I'd love to.' She smiled at him. 'Why don't you drop by my place one evening and I'll show you my range of designs? If it's her birthday next month, then there isn't enough time for me to design something specially for her and to make it from scratch, but you might find something suitable in my existing range.'

'Excellent! Thanks.' He looked at her, his eyes twinkling. 'I don't suppose Emma will be there when I come round, will she?'

'And there I was thinking it was me you were interested in.' She sighed.

'You didn't, did you?' Pete looked worried.

Her face broke into a grin. 'No, I didn't. I saw the way you two were looking at each other on Friday night. I can't think why you didn't ask her out then.'

'I wanted to, but . . . ' Pete paused as the waitress came over with their food and set the plates down on their table.

'Enjoy your meal.'

'Thank you,' Kendall told her. She looked inquisitively at Pete as the waitress walked away. 'But what?'

'I just couldn't seem to find the right moment. Besides, for all I know she might already have a boyfriend.'

'Luckily for you she hasn't.'

Emma had split up from her long-term boyfriend, Mark, a couple of months before, when she'd found out that he'd been unfaithful to her.

Another creep.

'And it just so happens that she's coming over tonight so why don't you drop in and see my jewellery then?'

'Thanks! I will.' Pete tucked into his meal with relish.

Kendall followed suit but somehow she didn't have much of an appetite. She kept picturing Jake lunching with the beautiful Leticia, and how she'd be flirting with him, clasping her hand over his.

Stop it, she told herself firmly. Anyone would think you were jealous.

Kendall pushed open the door of the office, stepped inside, and glanced through the glass partition into Jake's room, relieved to see that it was empty. Good, that meant she could be busy working — the polite, efficient secretary — when he came back from lunch.

She'd just begun replying to the e-mails on her screen when the telephone rang.

'Good afternoon, EXA Electronics. How can I help you?' she asked pleasantly.

'I need to speak to Mr Newman urgently.' The man spoke excellent English but she could tell from his accent that he was Spanish.

'I'm sorry, Señor, but Mr Newman is out of the office at the moment. Can I help?'

'When will he be back? It is imperative that I speak to him as soon as possible.' She could hear the anxiety in his voice. 'I have tried his mobile but it seems to be switched off.'

Obviously Jake didn't want to be disturbed.

'Could I ask who's calling, please?'

'Antonio Fernandez, from the Marbella office.'

'I'll give Mr Newman your message as soon as he returns, Señor Fernandez.'

'Gracias. Adios.'

She put down the receiver and looked at her watch. Half-past two. Joyce had told her that Jake was dedicated to his job and rarely took a lunch break. Yet Leticia turns up and he takes an extended one. Was Kendall jealous? Of course not. She shook her head vehemently.

'You'll frighten clients away with that scowl.' The voice was laced with amusement.

Startled, she looked towards the door. Jake was leaning nonchalantly against the doorframe, arms folded, his eyes twinkling.

'I didn't hear you come in!'

'Obviously.' He smiled engagingly and her heart did a triple somersault. Then he straightened up and walked over to her. 'Now tell me what's happened to put that frown on your face.'

You did. You and Leticia. 'Sorry, I didn't realise I was frowning. You've just had a call from the Marbella office and I was wondering how to contact you. Señor Fernandez said your mobile was switched off.'

He was instantly alert. 'Yes, I turned it off in the restaurant. I think it's appalling bad manners not to in a public place like that. Did Toni leave a message?'

'He said that it was imperative you called him as soon as possible.'

'I'll phone him now.' He was already on his way to his office. 'Bring me a coffee, will you, please?'

'Yes, of course.' She got up and walked over to the coffee machine. She pressed the button, then — while she waited for the coffee to percolate — she turned around to look through the glass partition at Jake.

He was sitting on a corner of his desk, his head bowed as he spoke into the receiver. He had a good profile, she thought; straight nose, strong jaw line.

As if sensing her scrutiny he glanced up and over at her. She felt herself flushing and turned around quickly, taking one of the china cups from the pile at the side of the machine and pouring coffee into it. Then she added a couple of drops of milk and one spoon of sugar, just as Joyce had told her he liked it. She stirred the coffee and was wondering whether to take it in to him, when he came out.

'Exactly how good is your Spanish?' he asked her.

'Well, I'm not exactly bilingual but I'm pretty fluent.'

'Good. I've got to go to Marbella for a couple of days and I need you to come with me.'

'Marbella? When?' she asked, her mind racing. Where would they be staying? She'd worked in Alicante on the Costa Blanca, and had visited Marbella and seen the luxury hotels there. It was the resort of the rich. She wasn't sure that her cheap and colourful wardrobe was up to it.

'As soon as possible. Tonight if we can get a flight.'

'Tonight? But Pete's coming round . . .' her voice trailed off as she saw his face tighten. Why had she said that? It wasn't that important. Pete could look at her jewellery designs — and get together with Emma — another time.

★　★　★

So she *was* going out with Pete now, thought Jake. Well, he hadn't wasted any time, had he? Still, why should he care? But he did care. He didn't want to think of her and Pete together, laughing, embracing . . . Darn it, Jake, pull yourself together, he told himself. You've got a business crisis to deal with and you haven't got time to be moping over some woman you've only just met.

60

'I'm sorry, but this is a very important business matter and I need a secretary with me,' he told her brusquely. 'Surely your boyfriend can do without you for a few days?'

He saw something flit across her face, but before he could make out what it was it was gone

'Of course. I'll come with you if it's that important,' she said coolly. 'I can cancel my arrangements for this evening. But I will need time to pack and get organised. How long will we be away for?'

'I'm not sure; until the weekend probably. Can you book two seats on the first available flight to Marbella? Just one way — we'll book a return flight while we're over there — then you can go home and pack. If you phone Joyce she'll tell you the password for our account with the local travel agent.'

'She told me this morning,' Kendall replied.

He watched as she switched screens to the Internet — like most firms they were permanently logged on — selected the travel operator, and keyed in a search for flights to Marbella. A few strands of her mahogany hair had escaped from the band she'd tied it back with, and he had to fight the urge to brush it from her face; to run his fingers over her creamy skin.

'There are no seats available from either Birmingham International or the East Midlands tonight,' she said, looking up at him. 'But there are seats on the eight o'clock flight from Birmingham International, tomorrow morning, arriving at Malaga airport just before ten o'clock Spanish time. Do you want me to book on that?'

'Yes, that will be ideal. Toni can meet us at the hotel when we arrive and fill me in on what's been happening over there.'

She selected the flights and waited for the screen to confirm the booking.

'We pick up the tickets at the airport,' she said. 'The latest boarding time is six-thirty.'

'Fine. Well, at least you won't need to cancel your precious date with Pete tonight.'

Ouch! There was no need for that, he told himself. No wonder she looks so startled. Lighten up, Jake. She's entitled to date anyone she wants.

'You'd better go home to give yourself time to pack.' He deliberately kept his tone friendly. 'I'll pick you up at half-past five tomorrow morning.'

She nodded. 'I presume you'll want hotel rooms booked, too?'

'Yes, better book two rooms until the weekend. I usually stay at Hotel Las Palmas — you'll find the number in the desk diary.'

She made notes and then looked up at him.

'What exactly have you got scheduled? Only, I'm not sure what clothes to take. It will be pretty hot over there. And I guess I'll need some formal wear?'

'Just pack a couple of business outfits and something for evenings,' he told her. 'If you need anything else you can buy it over there and put it on the business credit card.'

A slow smile played on her lips and he wondered if, like him, she was remembering the last time he'd given her his credit card. Was it really only three days ago? He felt as if he'd known her forever. Waited for her forever.

⋆ ⋆ ⋆

How am I going to cope alone with him in Spain for four days, Kendall thought in panic as she drove home.

They'd be thrown into each other's company so much and probably have to spend most of each day — and evening — together. She'd found the few hours she'd spent with him in the office awkward enough. Maybe that's why she'd let him believe Pete was her boyfriend, so that he'd lose interest in her.

Don't be stupid, she told herself; you don't even know if he is interested in you. But he is. I know he is. Anyway, this is a business trip. You'll be too busy working to bother about anything else. Besides, it's about time you got over this stupid crush you've got on Jake Newman. Stop acting like a love-struck teenager and get on with the job. Men like Jake are only interested in casual affairs and she wasn't that sort of girl, even if she wasn't interested in long-term commitment, either.

She fixed herself a light meal when she got home, then looked out her suitcase and packed a couple of business suits and co-ordinating shirts, three dresses suitable for evening wear, as Jake had suggested, and a couple of casual outfits. Then she carefully selected jewellery to go with the evening dresses.

She always wore her own designs. Apart from the fact that she liked to wear original jewellery, it was a good advertisement for her work.

She added a few pairs of shoes to her case, along with a couple of nightshirts and some underclothes, and was just wondering whether to take any beach-wear when the buzzer sounded to announce Emma's arrival.

'How's the new job with the gorgeous Jake?' she asked, as soon as she came into the flat — then did a double-take when she saw the half-packed suitcase on the bed, surrounded by most of the contents of Kendall's wardrobe. 'Don't tell me you're running away with him already? Talk about a fast worker!'

'Funnee!' Kendall picked up a pillow and threw it at her friend. 'If you must know, I'm going on a business trip with him to Spain.'

'A *business* trip?'

'Yes, business. Some sort of crisis has come up in the Marbella office and he has to fly over to sort it out. He needs me to go with him.'

'Why? Surely he can use one of the secretaries from the office over there if he needs to? I would have thought he'd leave you here to deal with things while he's away.'

Kendall had to admit that Emma had a point. She hadn't stopped to wonder why he'd wanted her to go to Spain with him or who was going to look after his office while they were both away.

'If you ask me it's just an excuse to get you alone,' Emma said mischievously.

Was it? Don't be stupid, of course it wasn't. He wanted her to go with him because she spoke Spanish, that was all.

'Yeah, right.' Kendall continued with her packing. 'And I suppose the fact that I can speak the language has nothing to do with it?'

'I reckon he's more interested in you than in your linguistic abilities. I saw the way he couldn't keep his eyes off you on Friday night.' Emma sat down on the bed and looked at the contents of the suitcase. 'You're not taking these with you!' she shrieked in horror.

'What?' Puzzled, Kendall looked around from hunting in the wardrobe for her grey, leather handbag.

'These naff nightshirts.' Emma took a

nightshirt out of the case and held it up. It was big, baggy and adorned with a picture of a cartoon kitten.

'What's wrong with my nightshirts? You wear nightshirts, too, I know you do.'

'Yes, but Kendy, you're going to Spain.' Emma said the words slowly.

'And what's that got to do with it?'

'Everything. You can't let Jake see you in these. You need to take something floaty and romantic to wear. Just in case.'

'Emma! Jake Newman will *not* be seeing me in my nightie. Not ever! Is that clear?'

'But what if there's a fire and you have to run out of your room in the middle of the night?' Emma pointed out. 'A girl should always be prepared.'

Before Kendall could reply the buzzer went again.

It must be Pete! Oops! She'd forgotten all about him.

'I'll be back in a minute,' she told Emma, hurrying out into the hall.

She pressed the button to open the main entrance for the second time that evening, then went out on to the landing to lean over the rail to look for Pete.

'I'm up here on the second floor,' she called.

He ran up the stairs two at a time to join her. 'Is Emma here, yet?' he asked anxiously.

'Yes, she arrived about ten minutes ago. Come on in.'

Emma was now in the living-room, posed casually on the sofa. Kendall had to admire the way she had arranged herself, flicking through the pages of a magazine, seemingly oblivious to their presence.

She glanced up as they walked in. 'Have you got another guest, Kendy? Should I go?' Then her blue eyes widened innocently as they rested on Pete. 'Oh, hello! Fancy meeting you again.'

'Hi, Emma!' He gave her the benefit of his most devastating smile.

He really was very good-looking, thought Kendall. Not in a hunky way, like Jake, but good-looking nonetheless. Oh goodness, there she was thinking of Jake again!

'Pete's come to look through my jewellery designs,' she told Emma. 'He wants something for his mum's birthday.' She turned to the door. 'Would you mind making him a cup of coffee while I just go and look out my samples?'

'Sure.' Emma got to her feet. 'How do you like your coffee, Pete?'

Kendall smiled to herself as she walked along the hall to her bedroom.

Something told her those two would get on fine. She glanced over at the open case on the bed — she'd have to finish her packing later. Still, most of it was done now.

* * *

Later, after Pete had admired Kendall's jewellery samples and had arranged for her to make a bracelet for his mum's birthday, he and Emma had left together, intending to go on to a wine bar for a drink and a chat.

They'd invited Kendall along, of course, but she'd refused, saying she had to finish her packing. Which was true. But even if she hadn't been flying to Marbella early the next morning, she still wouldn't have gone with them.

It was obvious they'd wanted to be alone to get to know each other better.

Part of her felt happy for Emma — she liked Pete and thought they would be good together — but part of her felt sad, knowing it would probably end in tears eventually, as so many relationships did.

It wasn't until she'd finished packing and had sat down to drink a mug of hot chocolate before she went to bed, that she noticed Pete's jacket on the back of the sofa. He must have been so wrapped up in Emma that he'd forgotten about it.

Knowing that she'd be away for a few

days, she was just wondering what to do about it when her mobile phone rang.

'Kendall?' It was Pete calling — she'd given him her mobile number in case he wanted to contact her about his mum's present. She didn't want him phoning the office again.

'I've left my jacket in your flat. Is it OK if I pop by for it first thing in the morning?'

'Sure, but I'm leaving for the airport at half-past five, remember?'

'Oh, yes. You did say. I forgot.' There was silence for a moment. 'OK, I'll just have to drag myself out of bed early to pick it up. I'll be there before you go.'

'Fine. See you . . . Oh, Pete?'

'Yes?'

'You and Emma really hit it off, didn't you?'

'Instant attraction, Kendy. How could she resist my charms?' He chuckled. 'Seriously, she's a real babe and we're going for a meal together tomorrow night.'

'Good. I'm pleased. See you in the morning, then.'

''Bye. And thanks. I owe you a big favour.'

Kendall had no sooner put down the phone than it rang again.

'Kendy, you'll never guess what?' It was Emma, sounding breathless and excited.

'I don't need to guess, I know. You've got a date with Pete tomorrow night. He's just told me. But I don't know all the details so come on, fill me in.'

Emma didn't need encouragement.

Almost an hour later, Kendall finally climbed into bed, exhausted. She longed for sleep but it eluded her. She tossed and turned all night, worrying how she was going to cope for four days with Jake Newman.

★ ★ ★

Jake hardly slept a wink all night, either. All he could think about was how he was going to cope in Spain for four days with Kendall McKenzie. He was finding it hard to keep his distance from her. It was ridiculous. He'd dated plenty of women but no-one had ever affected him this badly. Maybe that's what it had been like for his father.

Melanie, Jake's ex-stepmother, had been very beautiful and clever. And some years ago, lonely and vulnerable after his wife's death, Jake's father had fallen for her in a really big way. They'd had a whirlwind courtship and marriage, and then she'd shown her true colours. After she'd had several affairs, Jake's devastated father had finally divorced her, and she'd retaliated by taking him for every penny she possibly could.

The stress had caused his father to have a major heart attack, so Jake had given up his website design business and taken over the running of his father's company — EXA Electronics — which by that time had been so neglected that it was in danger of going into liquidation.

That had been five years ago, and Jake had built the business up into a successful international concern — and had put up a steel wall around his heart at the same time. There was no way he was going to fall for any woman and then let her trample all over his heart.

No commitment, that was Jake's motto and the women he went out with knew it.

Which was why Kendall scared him. She attracted him too much.

Don't be stupid, she's got a boyfriend already, he told himself, turning over and pummelling the pillow.

Anyway, she probably wasn't even interested in him. *But she was.* He could feel it. Even though, like him, she was fighting it. And she'd only been going out with that Pete character for a couple of days, so her relationship with him couldn't be that serious.

Which just shows how wrong you can be, thought Jake as, early the next morning, he watched Pete walk away from the block of flats where Kendall lived, his jacket slung casually over one shoulder.

Their relationship was obviously more serious than he'd realised.

I must be mad to be going to Spain with her, he thought. He didn't know what had possessed him to ask her to go with him in the first place — he usually borrowed one of the secretaries in the Marbella office and left Joyce in the UK to run the office over here. But he'd wanted to get to know her better and had used her knowledge of Spanish as an excuse.

Well, he realised now what a stupid decision it had been. He'd go and tell her that he didn't need her to come with him, after all. As far as he was concerned, the more distance he put between himself and Kendall McKenzie the better.

A Betrayal

'Come on up, I'm on the second floor!' Kendall shouted into the intercom as soon as Jake pressed the buzzer. 'Number 18, on the left. The door's on the latch.'

He pushed open the heavy entrance door to the flats and stepped inside. A quick glance showed him that there was no lift so he made his way up the stone steps. He scanned the numbers on the doors and found number 18.

'Hello? Kendall?'

'I'm in the living-room. Straight down the hall.'

He smiled as he stepped into the hall. Her flat might look the same as everyone else's on the outside, but she'd certainly made her mark on the inside.

Several eye-catching Chinese paintings decorated the walls, and when he entered the living-room he saw several oriental statues there that were more evidence of her travels. Of Kendall herself there was no sign.

'I'm in the kitchen, just making sure I've switched everything off.'

He turned and saw an open door leading into the kitchen where Kendall, her back towards him, was unplugging the kettle. She was wearing a neat, grey, pinstriped suit, the jacket tapering in at the waist and the skirt finishing just above the knee, with enough of a slit to reveal very shapely legs.

She turned around and smiled at him, and his heart missed a beat. She looked incredibly pretty and fresh, even at this early hour.

Her glowing hair was loosely tied back from her face, which looked bare of make-up apart from a touch of lipstick, and her eyes were bright and sparkling, as if she'd had a restful night's sleep.

'OK, I'm ready now. I've just got to get my suitcase out of the bedroom.'

This is where he was supposed to tell her that she was staying at the Birmingham office; that he didn't need her in Spain, after all. But the words wouldn't come. He might not need her in Spain with him but he definitely wanted her there.

Kendall took a deep breath as she went to fetch her case. Jake looked so handsome, in that dark-grey business suit, with that brooding look on his face, that she'd hardly been able to take her eyes off him.

She lifted her case off the bed and realised too late that it was heavier than she'd thought. She stumbled as she carried it out of the room and it banged against the back of her leg.

'Ouch!' The cry of pain was out before she could stop it. She put the case down and rubbed her throbbing calf, grimacing as she saw she had a ladder in her tights and that a bruise was already forming.

'Are you all right?' Jake's worried face appeared around the door. 'That looks nasty,' he said sympathetically.

She felt her cheeks grow hot under his scrutiny. 'I caught my leg on my case but I'll be fine. I just need to change my tights.'

'I'll wait in the car for you.' He walked along the hall and effortlessly picked up the heavy suitcase. 'And we're all right for a few minutes if you want to put some ice on that bruise.'

Without waiting for an answer, he carried the suitcase out of the front door.

Maybe the ice would be a good idea, Kendall thought wryly. The way he'd looked at her had certainly made her temperature rise.

Don't even think about him, she warned herself as she took a new pair of tights out of the drawer.

She'd better make sure she kept this Spanish trip strictly business because if she allowed it to be anything else she would be well out of her depth.

★　★　★

It was only as she walked into the car park at the back of the flats that Kendall realised she didn't know what sort of car Jake drove, but the sleek, midnight-blue Porsche just had to be his.

She was a bit taken aback when he got out, walked around and opened the passenger door for her. Not many guys did that nowadays.

'Thank you.' She smiled broadly at him as she got into the passenger seat.

'My pleasure.' There was a hint of teasing in his reply, as if he knew he'd surprised her.

'Nice car,' she said as he got in beside her.

'Thanks.' He flashed her a smile. 'I quite like it too.'

'It might have been better if you'd got someone to drop us off at the airport so they could take the car back,' she suggested. 'Are you leaving it there until we return?'

'No. I've left a spare set of keys with my chauffeur. He'll pick it up from the airport later this morning, then drive it home for me. It didn't seem fair to drag him out of bed this early.'

He's a nice guy, Kendall thought; kind and considerate yet rich and successful. In her experience the qualities didn't always mix.

As they drove along, she was acutely aware of his presence beside her; of his strong hands holding the wheel casually but firmly; of his left hand reaching down to change gear, effortlessly and smoothly, just a few centimetres from her knee.

'How long did you teach in Thailand?' he asked her. 'I spent a bit of time over there myself a couple of years ago. It's a beautiful country.'

'I was there for a year.' She was glad of the diversion. 'I taught in a school in Chiang Mai.'

For the rest of the journey they spoke about Thailand and some of the other countries they had both visited, and she realised that he was actually very easy to talk to, with a good sense of humour.

She was almost sorry when they arrived at the airport; she'd enjoyed his company so much.

Careful, she told herself. I bet he's as charming as this with all the women he meets. She knew he had a reputation for collecting beautiful girlfriends — Tanya had hinted as much at the engagement party. He was the eternal bachelor. Well, she was the eternal bachelor girl, wasn't she? She could handle Jake Newman, even if he did make her go all goose-bumpy.

★ ★ ★

Malaga Airport was crowded, as usual. Jake placed a hand on Kendall's elbow to guide her through the noisy throng as they walked through the arrivals hall, and she felt that now familiar tingle run up her arm and down her spine.

An employee from the Marbella office was there to meet them, and from the respectful way he spoke to Jake, Kendall gathered that her new boss was held in high regard. José, as the man was called, ushered them both into a very impressive silver Mercedes.

'Señor Fernandez sends his apologies, something urgent has come up that requires his attention. He will meet you at the hotel for lunch, Señor Newman,' Jose said in perfect English as he put the cases in the boot. 'He's booked a table for twelve-thirty.'

'Gracias.' Jake nodded approvingly.

* * *

As they pulled up outside the elegant and obviously very expensive Hotel Las Palmas, Kendall wondered just how highly regarded Jake was by EXA Electronics for them to put him up in such luxury. He seemed to be a regular client at the hotel and — if the smiles and deferential greetings in Spanish were anything to go by — he was held in very high esteem. She knew that he was a director, but his position at EXA Electronics was definitely far more influential than she had realised.

Kendall had several times visited Marbella and had seen the luxury hotels on the coast, but the Hotel Las Palmas exceeded her expectations.

From the marble floor of the foyer, to the exquisite chandeliers, the building oozed elegance.

Glancing around at the other guests — at the women immaculately made-up, and dressed in designer clothing — she felt distinctly out of place in her smart but nevertheless off-the-peg suit, and wished desperately that she'd put on a bit more make-up herself that morning.

'Relax, you look lovely,' Jake whispered, his mouth just a few centimetres away from her hair.

She screwed up her nose. 'Is it so obvious that I feel out of place?'

'Only to me. To everyone else you look a picture of sophistication.'

'Thanks. I just wish I felt it.'

'Would you like to be shown straight to your rooms, Señor Newman?' the porter asked. 'Your bags have already been taken up.'

Jake looked at Kendall. 'Would you like to see your room and freshen up before lunch?' he asked.

'Yes, please,' she told him. Already she was feeling hot and sticky, and she was curious to see if the bedrooms were as luxurious as the rest of the hotel.

'I presume I'm in my usual room?' Jake asked.

'Si, Señor, and the senhorita is next door to you, in room 110.'

'Then there's no need to escort us up. If you could just give me the keys, please.'

'Certainly.' The man walked over to the reception desk and came back with two keys.

'Gracias,' Jake thanked the man.

★   ★   ★

It was a beautiful room, Kendall thought as she stepped inside after Jake had insisted on opening the door for her, telling her he'd call for her in twenty minutes.

Decorated throughout in pastel-green and white, with pastel-green silk drapes and an elegant two-seater sofa in the same shade, it looked like something out of a glossy lifestyle magazine.

Her case had been placed by the side of the bed, which was covered with a delicately embroidered white throw-over.

She began to unpack. There wasn't time to put everything away but she was anxious to hang up her suits and evening dresses before they creased.

She smiled as she noticed that her nightshirts had disappeared from the case, and that the white, lacy nightdress with the matching wrap, that Emma had bought her last Christmas had been put in their place.

Trust Emma! She must have done that when Kendall had left the room to let in Pete.

She held up the nightie; it was really

pretty — with lace straps, a fitted bodice and a long, floaty, layered skirt. So pretty that she'd been reluctant to wear it.

But maybe her friend was right; if she was staying in a posh hotel in Spain then she should have some decent nightgear!

Thankfully, Emma hadn't swapped anything else, although she had added a slinky black evening dress. Kendall had bought it in Madrid and had never yet been anywhere special enough to wear it. It was the sort of dress that made you look as if you'd been poured into it.

Honestly, Emma was incorrigible!

Once her clothes were hung up, Kendall went through to the bathroom.

This was another gorgeous room, with pastel-green marble tiles and a jacuzzi in the corner. If only she had time to use that jacuzzi!

She was just freshening up her lipstick when Jake knocked on the door.

'Are you ready to go down to lunch?'

'Won't be a minute!'

She blotted her lips and studied herself in the mirror. She looked a bit tired, which was only to be expected after her late night and early start. Still, she'd do. Grabbing her handbag, she headed for the door.

★ ★ ★

Antonio Fernandez was already seated at a table and he stood up as they approached, greeting them both in perfect English.

'Toni, this is Kendall McKenzie, my secretary,' Jake introduced her as they sat down.

'Pleased to meet you,' Toni told her, then turned to Jake and remarked in Spanish how lucky he was to have such a beautiful secretary.

'Gracias, Señor,' Kendall thanked him mischievously, revealing that she'd understood what he'd said.

Antonio flushed and Jake smiled. 'Miss McKenzie speaks pretty good

Spanish which is why I brought her with me! Now, let's order something to eat and you can tell me what's been going on.'

Over lunch, Toni explained the problem.

'We've lost a few small contracts over the past months,' he said, frowning. 'Then a couple of weeks ago we lost a really big contract and now we're in danger of losing the Mendez business.'

Surprise registered on Jake's face. 'But we've always dealt with Benedicto Mendez.' He took a sip of his orange juice before asking, 'Is someone undercutting us?'

'Yes, and I don't think it's luck. I think that someone from within the company is leaking vital information to our rivals.'

Jake's face darkened. 'Have you any idea who?'

Toni shook his head. 'But I do know that every contract we've lost has gone to the same firm, Clavero Sistemas.'

'Clavero Systems? They've only been

going for a couple of years! And they're getting our contracts?' Jake was instantly alert. 'You're right, Toni, someone must be leaking information to them and when I find out who it is . . . ' He left the sentence unfinished. 'Does my father know about this?'

'No, he is still in Switzerland so I thought it best to speak to you first.'

Jake nodded. 'You did the right thing. I'll deal with this. I don't want my father bothered.'

Kendall listened to the exchange between the two men in silence, wondering again just how important a role Jake played in the firm. Important enough for him to be brought over to Spain to sort out trouble, she thought. And it seemed that his father was a bigwig in EXA Electronics too. Then it dawned on her; his father must own the company.

That's why Jake had been called in to sort things out; his father was away so he had to take charge. No wonder they'd sent a chauffeur-driven car and he stayed in such a posh hotel. Jake Newman was one seriously rich and important man.

'I'll contact Benedicto Mendez today and see if I can salvage the contract,' he was saying now. 'Meanwhile, I want a list of anyone who's joined the staff in the last few months and a list of all the contracts we've lost over the same period.'

Toni nodded. 'The lists will be on your desk within the hour.'

'Maybe the information isn't being leaked on purpose,' Kendall butted in.

Both men stared at her.

'What do you mean?' Jake asked.

'Maybe someone's been talking to a . . . friend,' she faltered, 'and that friend is passing it on but the first person doesn't know that.'

It had happened to Emma once. She'd carelessly leaked some information to a boyfriend who had passed it on. Emma had almost lost her job because of it.

'I didn't think of that. You could be

right. Someone from Clavero could have deliberately befriended a member of staff to use them as a source of information.' Jake turned to Toni. 'What sort of personal details do you have on record about the staff?'

'We know who's married and who isn't, but that's about it,' Toni replied. 'I've no idea who's seeing who, although I bet the secretaries know all the gossip.'

'Of course they do!' A light dawned in Jake's eyes as he looked at Kendall. 'I want you to keep your ears open when we're at the office,' he told her, 'and if you hear anything about anyone who has a connection with Clavero's, please let me know.'

'No problem,' she told him. She could understand his anger. If someone was leaking information, even unknowingly, the future of the company and all its staff was in jeopardy.

Jake glanced at his watch. 'It's almost siesta time,' he said, referring to the Spanish tradition of taking a three-hour break in the afternoon to escape from the heat of the sun. 'So I'll have plenty of time to look through the files while the majority of the staff are out of the way. Can you call a meeting for five o'clock when they all return, Toni?'

'Si, Señor Newman. I will phone the office now and arrange it. If you will excuse me?'

He left the table to make his phone call.

It seemed like it was going to be a long day, Kendall thought, stifling a yawn. She wouldn't mind a siesta herself.

'Are you tired?' Jake's voice was soft, almost caring.

She looked at him and smiled. 'Oh, dear, does it show that much? I'm afraid I didn't get much sleep last night. I'll just go and freshen myself up before we leave, if that's OK?'

'Sure, take your time.'

Jake watched her as she walked away, leaving the words, 'I didn't have much sleep last night,' ringing in his head. The memory of Pete leaving her flat early that morning flashed through his mind and he felt a surge of jealousy. Get a grip, he told himself curtly. You've enough on your hands sorting out this business without drooling over a woman. Especially one who's involved with someone else.

'Where is la bella señorita McKenzie?' Toni asked as he returned to the table.

'Gone to freshen up,' Jake told him. 'And don't get any ideas of chatting her up, Toni. She's spoken for.'

'Si, I can tell she is your lady, Señor Newman, but I am surprised. It's not like you to get involved with staff. Still, she is so beautiful.'

He shrugged his shoulders as if dismissing Jake's temporary lapse.

'I'm not involved with her. Whatever gave you that idea?' Jake said curtly. 'She has a boyfriend in England.'

Toni looked surprised. 'But the way you look at each other . . . ' his voice trailed off as Kendall returned.

'Sorry to keep you waiting,' she said, dazzling them both with her smile. 'I'm ready to go now.'

What did Toni mean, Jake thought as he stood up to leave — the way they looked at each other? Was his attraction for Kendall so obvious? And even more interesting, was she attracted to him? Don't be daft, he told himself.

'We'll all go in your car, Toni,' he said. 'I'll arrange for mine to be taken out of the garage and brought to the office.'

*　*　*

What a day! Kendall thought, when they were finally driven back to the hotel that evening. After spending the entire afternoon at the office, they'd returned to the hotel for a quick shower and to change before going on to one of Marbella's exclusive beachside restaurants to have dinner with Benedicto Mendez and his wife.

During the meal, Benedicto had

revealed that Clavero Sistemas had undercut EXA Electronics in a bid for a software contract, which is why he was considering giving them all his business.

Jake, all smooth talk and charm, had promised to meet Clavero's bid and so had saved the contract, but Kendall had sensed his carefully controlled anger and now, sitting beside him on the back seat of the chauffeur-driven limousine, his fury was almost tangible. She wanted to reach out to touch his face and stroke the tension away.

'I guess this kind of thing goes on a lot in business,' she ventured, 'but at least you've got the contract back.'

'If there is one thing I detest, Kendall, it's betrayal.' He turned to look at her, his brown eyes dark with anger. 'I expect loyalty from my employees, not treachery. When I find out who is behind this they will regret it, I promise you.'

He would be a tough enemy, she realised. She had only ever seen the easy-going Jake up until now, and yet she had to admit he was right to be angry — someone was costing the company thousands, if not millions of pounds. She wondered if his views on betrayal extended to his personal life. Would he be so angry if a girlfriend betrayed him with another man? But then, what woman would want another man if she had Jake?

'Penny for them? Or should I say euros since we're in Spain?'

'Sorry?' she said, startled.

'You were miles away. I was offering you a penny for your thoughts.'

She felt her cheeks flush at the very idea of Jake knowing that she'd been thinking about him. 'I was just wondering if I'd have time to visit my parents while I'm here,' she replied quickly. 'They live in Antiquera.'

'Of course you must visit them,' he insisted. 'In fact, you can take one of the company cars and drive over tomorrow afternoon, at siesta time. I'm going to be in a meeting and it isn't necessary for you to be there. Would that suit you?'

'That would be lovely, thank you,' she said, smiling.

She'd ring her parents first thing in the morning to make sure they'd be in. She didn't want to go all that way and miss them. She knew they had a busy social life.

She yawned again as the car pulled up outside the hotel. 'Sorry,' she apologised, 'but I can hardly keep awake.'

'Then I won't ask you to join me for a nightcap at the bar,' Jake told her. 'I can see that you'd much prefer your bed.'

'Aren't you tired?' she asked him. After all, he'd had an early start, too, and had been working hard all day.

'A little,' he confessed. 'But there are a couple of things I still need to do.'

The chauffeur opened the door for her and she stepped out into the cool, night air.

Jake thanked the driver and they both

walked into the hotel.

As they picked up their room keys, the receptionist handed Jake an envelope.

'There have been several messages for you, Señor Newman,' she said. 'I've written them down for you.'

'Gracias.'

He smiled as he took the note from her, and from the besotted look she gave him, Kendall knew that the poor girl was smitten.

He must have broken so many hearts.

Well, she was going to make sure that he didn't break hers.

A Wonderful Opportunity

Knowing that they were early risers, Kendall telephoned her parents before she left for work to let them know she would be over to see them that afternoon, and they were delighted, as they always were when she visited.

She'd just put the phone down, and had gone over to the mirror to finish putting on her make-up, when a knock on the door made her jump and smudge her lipstick.

'Are you ready, Kendall?' It was Jake.

'Almost.'

She dabbed the smear of lipstick off her cheek with a tissue, reapplied it, then surveyed her reflection.

She looked a bit dark under the eyes, thanks to a sleepless night thinking about her boss, but there was nothing she could do about that. Picking up her bag she headed for the door.

Jake was charm itself, and the short drive passed in idle chit-chat about Spain and Kendall's parents.

Once they got to the office, he gave her a pile of paperwork to check over relating to the Mendez contract, and then he went off to a meeting.

She was relieved to have a bit of space from him; being so close to him in the car had put her nerves on edge. What was it about the guy that got under her skin?

He came back to the office at lunch time to pick up the contract.

'There's a car ready and waiting in the car park for you,' he said, handing her a set of keys, then perched on the edge of her desk.

She looked at the key fob and raised her eyebrows when she saw the word *Mercedes* embossed upon it.

'Is there a problem?' His tone was light and teasing.

She looked up. He was smiling at her.

'No problem at all,' she told him, teasing him back. 'I was expecting a

BMW but a Mercedes will just have to do, I suppose!'

He leaned across and touched her hand. 'Drive carefully. I don't need to remind you what Spanish roads are like.'

She could feel the heat rising up her arm from his touch but didn't pull her hand away.

'I'm not sure that you can actually call them roads in Antiquera, at least not where my parents live,' she told him, fighting to keep her voice level. 'Are you sure you haven't got an older car you want me to take? Those mountain tracks can be a bit basic.'

'Which is why I want you to have a reliable car. I need you for another business meeting tonight, so I can't afford to run the risk of you breaking down.'

'You're all heart.' She gently eased her hand from under his. 'Now, I'd better get going if you want me back for dinner. My parents will have a heavy lunch laid out for me, an album of photos to show me, and lots of questions to ask. The sooner I get there the better.'

He stood up. 'See you later then. We're meeting Señor Olaiz and his wife at the restaurant at nine o'clock so I'll call for you at eight-thirty. OK?'

'Fine. I'll be back in plenty of time,' she promised.

Watching him walk out of the room, she felt a fleeting pang of regret that he wasn't coming with her. Yeah, and you know what your parents would make of that, she told herself. They'd think the two of you were an item.

But I wouldn't mind.

The words came uninvited into her mind and she instantly swatted them away. She didn't need or want a man. All men did was complicate your life and break your heart. What she wanted was to save enough money to get herself a little workshop and start her own jewellery business.

What she didn't want was a 'love 'em and leave 'em' guy like Jake messing with her emotions. Definitely not.

104

Her parents lived in a restored finca — a small villa — high up in the mountains. They'd fallen in love with Spain after many holidays there, had spotted the finca when visiting friends, and had decided to retire to the sun when her father was offered redundancy.

As she turned off the motorway and took the road up to the untamed beauty of the mountains, Kendall felt tempted to join them in Spain permanently.

She'd always loved the Spanish way of life, the long siestas, the friendliness of the people and, of course, the sun. She'd thought about staying on when her previous teaching contract had ended, but England still felt like home and her flat and friends were there, so she'd returned to the UK.

★ ★ ★

The tarmac road finally led to the picturesque Spanish village where her

105

parents went to buy their bread and daily supplies, then suddenly gave way to the dirt track that led up into the mountains and to their home.

As Kendall approached their cottage, she could see them sitting in the garden, a jug of freshly-squeezed orange juice — from their own orange trees — on the table in front of them.

Although they loved Spain and had many friends there, her parents still missed their friends and family in England and were always delighted when Kendall came over to visit. They stood up and waved as she parked, then her father started walking to meet her.

'Nice car,' he told her, looking it over admiringly.

'It belongs to my boss. I think he's got a whole fleet of them.'

'Well, it looks like you've got yourself a good job this time.' He gave her a welcoming hug. 'A room at one of the most exclusive hotels on the Costa and the loan of a top of the range Mercedes. Can't be bad!'

'I know, and I only started working for Jake on Monday!'

'Jake?' he asked as they walked over to join her mother.

'Jake Newman, my new boss.'

'Two days and you're already on first name terms with him?' Her mother gave her a sideways look. 'Would you like a glass of orange juice?' She indicated the jug. 'It's just out of the fridge.'

'Thanks, I'd love one.' Kendall kissed her mum and sat down on the chair beside her. 'I met Jake at Tanya and Hugh's engagement party. He asked me to fill in for his secretary who's off work with a broken ankle,' she explained.

It would only complicate things if she told them how she'd almost knocked him down with Sophie's pushchair earlier that day. Knowing her mother's fertile imagination she'd jump to the conclusion that he'd fallen in love with her at first sight, attended the party because he'd hoped she would be there, and offered her the job because he couldn't bear to lose her.

'Well, I'm so pleased you took him up on his offer; it's lovely to see you again,' her mother told her as she poured her juice.

'It's nice to be back here.' Kendall sat back in her chair and stretched.

'I don't know why you don't come to live here. You could sell your flat and stay with us until you got a job and found a place of your own. Your father and I would be delighted to have you. Wouldn't we, John?'

'Of course we would. Why don't you think about it, Kendy? Come back over here when this temping job is finished. It's time you settled down and had a permanent base instead of flitting around the world. I know you've got your flat but you rent it out more than you live in it.'

Kendall sipped her orange juice as she thought how to tactfully word her reply.

She loved her parents to bits but there was no way she could live with them!

She was used to her independence now, coming and going as she pleased.

However, the idea of living in Spain did appeal to her. Especially living here on the Costa del Sol. She'd enjoyed her teaching job in Madrid but preferred southern Spain. And if she moved in with her parents her living costs would be so little that maybe she could finally concentrate on her jewellery business.

No, it wouldn't work out, she told herself. They'd soon be driving each other mad.

'It's a nice idea, but I'd need a place of my own. When I've saved enough money I want to take the plunge and concentrate on my jewellery designs full-time.'

'You could always buy that little finca near the village,' her mother suggested. 'It needs a bit of work but your dad would help you and there's a workshop too, where you could make your jewellery.'

'And you could get a job teaching English in Marbella until you'd saved enough money to give up work,' her father added.

'How much is this finca?' Kendall asked, out of curiosity more than anything else.

She couldn't believe it when her father told her the price. If she sold her flat, and scrimped and scraped, she might just be able to afford it.

It was a wonderful idea!

And if she could make jewellery full-time it would be her dream come true.

'I guess I could have a look.'

'We'll take you down there after lunch. If Maria's in she'll show you around,' her mother told her. 'I'm sure she'd accept a lower price. She's a widow who's anxious to sell because she's buying a flat in town near her daughter.'

★   ★   ★

So, after a delicious, fluffy omelette and a cup of fresh coffee, they all set off to see the finca.

110

Her father insisted on taking his car and doing the driving.

Kendall smiled to herself as she got into the back seat. Strange how you could be an independent adult, holding down a responsible job, living by yourself and travelling the world, yet as soon as you visited your parents you were back to being a child again.

Her father drove down the mountain track, stopping outside a pretty little lemon-coloured villa just the other side of the village.

'This is it,' he announced. 'And the front door's open so Maria must be home. That means you can have a look inside.'

Kendall stepped out of the car and looked around at the glorious untamed countryside. The little house was really in an ideal situation: close enough to the village if she needed anything, with neighbours only a short distance away and her parents within fifteen minutes drive; but isolated enough for her to have privacy. It was small — two

111

bedrooms her father had told her as they drove down — and a bit shabby, but that could soon be fixed.

An elderly Spanish lady came out and waved to them.

'Hola,' she called.

Her parents returned the greeting, then her mother explained, in Spanish, that Kendall was interested in buying the finca and asked if she could take a look inside.

'Si, si.' The woman nodded eagerly.

Kendall fell in love with the house as soon as she stepped through the door.

The rooms were small but had an old-fashioned charm. Sun streamed in through the windows, illuminating the whitewashed walls which were decorated with photos of the old lady's family. The rooms were cluttered, making them seem smaller than they were, but Kendall could see that it was more than big enough for her needs.

'It needs a coat of paint, of course,' her mother whispered. 'But that won't take long. It's in much better condition than our place was when we moved in.'

Maria led them upstairs, showing them around the two bedrooms and the tiny, but adequate, bathroom, all the time chattering away in Spanish.

'Could we see the garden too?' Kendall asked her.

'Si,' Maria said as she led them outside.

It was quite a large garden, with a couple of orange and lemon trees and a good-sized outbuilding tucked away at the far end.

Kendall felt a surge of excitement as she looked inside the workshop. At the moment it was full of rubbish but she could see that once it was cleared out and painted it would be ideal for her jewellery making.

'Well? Are you interested?' her father asked.

'It's lovely, but I'll have to think about it. It would be a huge financial commitment for me and I don't want to make a rushed decision.'

'Let's see if she'll come down in price

a bit,' he suggested.

Speaking slowly in Spanish, he told Maria that Kendall was interested in the finca but that it was a bit too expensive for her. Would she accept a lower price?

Maria replied that, for the sake of a quick sale, she would — naming a figure quite a bit below the original asking price.

Kendall almost said she'd buy it there and then!

At that price, after selling her flat, and with the savings she already had, she could afford to redecorate the house and be able to take some time off work to concentrate on her jewellery.

True, she would still need a small mortgage which would be difficult to get, seeing as she wouldn't have a job. But her father had offered to stand as guarantor for that, and she had enough saved to meet the repayments for a while — after which time she hoped to be making a reasonable income from her new business.

She thanked Maria and told her she would let her know as soon as possible.

★   ★   ★

'What do you think?' her father asked when they were once again back at her parents' home.

'I love it,' she told him. 'But I don't want to do anything hasty.'

'Why not go ahead and try it for a year?' her mother suggested. 'It would be just the same as if you were living abroad, teaching. If it doesn't work out you can always sell up and go back to England.'

'But I wouldn't have my flat to go back to,' she reminded her. The flat was her security.

'OK, rent your flat out as usual,' her father told her, 'and take out a bigger mortgage. The rent payments will meet the mortgage payments over here and I'll lend you the money to do up the finca. You can pay me back when you can, or when you sell up if you decide to go back to England.'

She did a quick calculation. She would still have enough savings to live for a year if she was careful. Like her mother said, what had she got to lose?

Jake.

The thought flashed across her mind before she could stop it.

She wouldn't be able to see Jake.

And a good thing, too, the way you're mooning over him, she told herself.

Besides, she was only working for him for a few weeks. And it would be much easier to forget about him if she was starting a new life in another country rather than still living in the same town as him back home in England.

'Thanks, Dad. It's really kind of you and I might take you up on it,' she said. 'Just give me a few days to think about it.'

'OK,' he told her. 'Take your time. Wait until you get back to England. I can always make an offer for the finca on your behalf.'

'You're staying with us for dinner,

aren't you?' her mother asked. 'We could go down to the restaurant in the village.'

'Sorry, Mum. I've to go with my boss to meet clients for dinner,' Kendall told her. 'In fact, I've got to head back to Marbella soon.'

★ ★ ★

As she drove back to the city, Kendall's thoughts were on the finca. It was what she'd always dreamed of — her own home with a workshop where she could make her jewellery and, with her parents' help, she might be able to make that dream come true. Shouldn't she grab at the opportunity?

But what about Jake?

What about him? He was her boss, and a temporary one at that.

He could be more than that.

As the thought flashed across her mind she knew, deep down, that this was true. She'd felt it as soon as she'd first set eyes on him. And she knew he felt the same.

She grimaced as a car shot past her, almost forcing her off the road.

She had to stop thinking about Jake and the finca and concentrate on her driving if she wanted to get back to Marbella in one piece.

★ ★ ★

Glancing at her watch as she hurried into the hotel, she saw that she still had time for a relaxing soak in the bath before getting ready for dinner.

She picked up her room key from reception and made her way over to the lift. Just as she reached it the doors opened and out stepped Jake and Leticia, arm in arm, laughing together.

'Oh, hi! Did you have a good afternoon?' Jake asked her.

'Fine, thank you,' she replied, trying not to notice the smug smile on Leticia's face as the glamorous blonde hung on tightly to his arm.

'Good, well, I'll call for you at half-past eight then. The restaurant is only a few minutes away.'

'OK.' She nodded and stepped into the lift.

'I wish you didn't have that boring business dinner this evening, darling,' she heard Leticia purr as they walked away. 'I was hoping you and I could go somewhere ourselves.'

The lift doors closed before Kendall could hear Jake's reply.

So much for her belief that Jake was interested in *her*.

And so much for his secretary Joyce's assertion that he was trying to shake off Leticia.

He obviously couldn't bear to be away from her even for a few days if he'd arranged for her to join him over here on his business trip!

Well, what if he had? It was nothing to do with Kendall. He was her boss, that was all.

Face it, Kendy, he might fancy you a bit, but Leticia's in his league and you're not.

And Kendall didn't want to be.

She didn't need any complications in her life.

She had a chance to follow her dream and she was going to grab it with both hands.

Tomorrow she would have another look at the finca and put in an offer for it.

Like her father had always told her, you had to take your chances when they came in life.

The Traitor Is Revealed

As soon as she'd had her bath, Kendall phoned her parents, asking her father to make enquiries about a mortgage and telling them that she was definitely interested in the finca. She promised to drive over as soon as she could for another look at it so that she could finally make up her mind.

'You're doing the right thing,' her father said. 'It's time you settled down and thought about the future. You can't travel the world for ever.'

He was right, she thought, putting down the receiver. This would be a good move for her.

So why did her heart feel so heavy?

She walked over to the window and looked out at the beach and the clear, blue sea that gently lapped against the shore. It was a romantic setting, and she wondered if Jake and Leticia were gazing out at the ocean together, their arms wrapped around each other.

Annoyed that her mind had once again begun to drift in such a direction she turned away from the window, shrugging her shoulders and glancing at the clock.

It was getting late. She'd better get ready to go down to dinner.

She'd brought three evening dresses with her and decided to wear the white one that draped over one shoulder and emphasised the tan she still had from working in northern Spain.

She teamed it with a crystal necklace and matching crystal drop earrings.

Simple but effective.

★ ★ ★

The dinner went well. Both charming and efficient, Jake soon convinced the client, Dino Olaiz, to give EXA Electronics the contract for installing software on all the new computers in the Olaiz offices in Barcelona.

This was another contract that had been about to go to Clavero's.

Jake was an excellent businessman.

Kendall had watched his performance throughout the evening. He gave nothing away, kept his cool, and was completely confident about his company's abilities.

She was in no doubt that he would find out who was leaking information and that that person would be very sorry indeed.

★   ★   ★

'Well, that's the second contract you've saved in less than two days,' she said as they got into the back of the chauffeured limousine. 'No wonder Toni was anxious for you to come over and save the company.'

'Thank you.' His voice was silky soft as he turned to face her, his warm brown eyes looking directly into hers.

She caught her breath and for a

moment time stood still as she returned his gaze.

The man was charm personified.

He'd had Dino Olaiz eating out of his hand and now he was looking at her as if he really cared about her; as if there was something between them.

He probably thought all he had to do was give her that smouldering look and she would go weak at the knees. Well, she wasn't going to fall for it.

She turned her head slightly so that she wasn't looking directly at him.

'Well, it's true,' she said, keeping her voice light and conversational.

'You must have saved the company a considerable amount of money in the short time you've been here. Are you any nearer to finding out who's been leaking information to your rivals?'

It was as if a dark shadow had fallen across his face, and he replaced the smiling, caring expression with a cold, unfeeling one. His eyes were like ice and his mouth was set in a rigid line.

'You know who it is, don't you?' she asked softly.

She saw the ice in his eyes start to melt.

'Let's just say that I've got a very good idea, and that they will regret it.'

'I bet they will. I feel sorry for anyone who crosses you. I wouldn't dare!'

'I think you would dare anything, Kendall McKenzie.' His voice was laced with amusement. 'However, I don't think dishonesty is one of your traits.'

'No, it isn't,' she said firmly. 'I would never, ever betray anyone.'

Was she thinking of Pete, Jake wondered, as he saw the spark of defiance in her lovely emerald eyes; was she telling him she knew he was attracted to her and warning him off? If so, she had nothing to worry about — he wasn't into stealing other men's girlfriends.

'My feelings exactly,' he agreed.

There — they had both made their positions clear.

So now they could just get on with their working relationship.

* ★ ★

Kendall let herself into her room, sat down on the bed, took off her shoes and wriggled her toes. Her feet had been killing her all evening but she was pleased she'd worn her strappy sandals. They'd gone well with her dress and had made her feel elegant. Something she'd definitely wanted to feel when they'd walked back into the hotel and found the luscious Leticia dolled up to the nines and waiting for Jake.

Leticia had dismissed Kendall with a nod and greeted Jake with a kiss on the cheek, then linked her arm possessively through his and led him off to the bar.

Jake, of course, had offered to see Kendall to her room first, but she'd told him there was no need; so, after arranging to pick her up for work in the morning, he had gone off with Leticia.

Not that she cared. Why should she?

After work tomorrow she'd drive over and have another look at the finca, make sure it was what she wanted, then put in an offer.

Her father would deal with all the paperwork on this side when she returned home.

Then, once Joyce was back at work, Kendall could rent out her flat and move over to live with her parents until the purchase of the finca had gone through.

She felt a surge of excitement at the knowledge that she would soon be embarking on a new life.

Feeling recharged, she decided she'd have a quick shower, then work on a few more jewellery designs before she went to bed.

As usual, once she started sketching, time sped by. She'd covered three pages with designs before fatigue overcame her and, glancing at the clock, she saw that it was past midnight.

Better get some sleep if you want to be bright and alert for work tomorrow, she told herself, putting the designs away.

But her sleep was disturbed by

thoughts of the finca.

And of Jake.

What is it with me, she thought ruefully as she tossed and turned in the middle of the night. I haven't known the guy for a week and I can't get him out of my mind.

The sooner she stopped working for him the better.

★   ★   ★

Jake seemed very preoccupied as he drove her to work the next morning. He hardly said two words to her, then, when they arrived at the office, he told her he would be in meetings all morning but that she'd find paperwork waiting for her that he wanted her to deal with.

'Are we having a business dinner again this evening?' she asked him.

'I'm afraid so. We're dining with a new client, Claude Tabaras and his wife. It's his contract you'll be working on this morning.'

He slowed the car, signalled left and took the road leading to the office.

'He has computer firms all over the world so this will be a lucrative contract for us if we can get the costings right.'

He parked the car, unfastened his seat belt, then turned to look at her.

'Why, is it a problem?'

'Of course not, that's what you pay me for,' she told him. 'It's just that I'd like to visit my parents again before we go back to England and I wondered when would be the best time to go.'

'Why don't you go this afternoon, at siesta, like yesterday?'

'Are you sure? You won't be needing me?'

'I can't expect you to work all day and evening,' he replied. 'Besides, I won't be in the office myself — I'm meeting Leticia.'

'That's OK then,' she said.

She opened the car door and got out quickly, hoping that her feelings didn't show on her face.

'I'll arrange for you to have the

Mercedes again,' he told her, locking the car doors. 'I'll leave it in the car park. You can pick up the keys from reception.'

'Thank you,' she said gratefully.

* * *

Toni was waiting for them outside Jake's office.

'How did it go last night?' he asked.

'We got the contract,' Jake told him.

'I knew you could swing it.'

'I'm not going to stand by and see the firm go under because one of our employees can't keep their mouth shut,' Jake said, grimly.

Toni looked surprised. 'Do you know who it is?'

'I've got a fairly good idea.' Jake looked around. 'Is Luis in yet?'

'No, but he's due at any minute. Why?'

'Ask him to come straight to my office, will you?'

Kendall gave Toni a sympathetic

smile and followed Jake along the corridor. He was walking briskly. Did he suspect Luis, or did he want to question him about another member of staff? She wondered who the culprit could be. She'd tried to keep her ears open but the staff knew she was Jake's PA and were careful not to gossip around her.

A very worried-looking Luis arrived five minutes later and the two men spent the entire morning in Jake's office.

Kendall was kept busy answering phone calls, dealing with e-mails and typing various letters and contracts, so the morning passed swiftly.

When Luis finally emerged, looking pale and drained, she was amazed to realise he'd been with Jake for over two and a half hours.

'Are you all right?' she asked him, concerned.

He shot her a panicky look and left without replying.

Surely he wasn't the traitor? She

didn't know Luis but she'd got the impression that he was a friendly, likeable man. She could hardly believe that he was the sort of person who'd betray the company he worked for.

A few minutes later, Jake buzzed for her to go through to his office.

'I'm going to be out for the rest of the day,' he told her as she walked into the room. 'Could you finish preparing the contract and then leave it on my desk? I'll pick it up later.'

'Of course.' She looked at him but his expression gave nothing away. 'Are you any nearer to finding out who's been giving away the company's secrets?'

'Oh, yes. It will all be sorted out today.'

Only the grim look in his eyes gave any hint of his anger.

She wanted to ask him if Luis was involved but something told her not to.

Jake was obviously very upset and angry about this whole business and would tell her in his own time if he wanted her to know.

And if he didn't tell her, was that surprising? He'd only known her a few days and she was only a temporary secretary.

It was really none of her business.

Realising that he was still looking at her, waiting for her to leave the room, she said briskly. 'That's good. I'll see you later.' And she turned and went out, trying to ignore the feeling that he was staring after her.

A few minutes later, he came through to her office.

'You can reach me on my mobile if you need me,' he told her, 'but please only contact me in an emergency. I'll call for you a bit earlier tonight so that we can discuss a few things before dinner. Shall we say at eight o'clock?'

'That's fine,' she told him. 'And Jake . . . good luck.'

For a moment his eyes held hers and she felt almost giddy.

'Thank you,' he told her. 'But luck doesn't come into it.'

No, it probably doesn't, she thought

as she watched him walk away.

Even from behind he looked incredibly sexy, especially in that fitted suit that emphasised his broad shoulders.

Oh, stop drooling, she told herself firmly.

★ ★ ★

Kendall's parents both went with her for another look at Maria's finca.

'Now, are you absolutely certain this is the house for you?' her father asked. 'We can get in touch with an estate agent to view a few other properties, if you want?'

She shook her head. 'No need, this is exactly what I'm looking for.'

'You're getting a bargain.' Her father's eyes were twinkling and she knew that he was delighted with her decision. 'I'll let Maria know right away and ask Brian to help us with the negotiations.'

Brian was one of their neighbours who spoke very fluent Spanish.

'Thanks, Dad.'

Half an hour later, Brian had arranged for a financial advisor to deal with the mortgage arrangements and for a solicitor to deal with the legal side.

There was certainly something to be said for having parents who lived in the country you wanted to move to, Kendall thought, as she drove back to the hotel later that afternoon.

★ ★ ★

It was a lovely little house, she told herself as she showered before dinner that evening, and it was a dream come true for her to have the opportunity to start her own business. She was delighted. And as for living in a completely different country to Jake. So what? She'd only met him a few days ago.

She pushed all thoughts of him to the back of her mind, rinsed her hair and turned off the shower. There was no time for daydreaming — he would be here for her soon.

She'd just finished dressing, this time in a turquoise, fitted top with a matching floaty skirt that skimmed her knees, when he rang her on her mobile.

'I'm going to be late, Kendall, so I've ordered a car to pick you up to take you to the restaurant. Can you entertain Claude Tabaras and his wife until I get there?'

'There's nothing wrong, is there?' she asked. Even over the phone she could tell that he was tense.

'Nothing at all. Thanks. I won't be long. I promise.'

Before she could ask anything else he had gone.

It wasn't like him to be so abrupt, but perhaps he was still dealing with whoever had been leaking information. She didn't envy him the task. It couldn't be a pleasant one.

A call from hotel reception at eight o'clock informed her that her car had arrived and she was pleased to see that it was the same driver that they'd had previously. It made her feel more relaxed — she was already feeling jittery about entertaining a VIP Spanish client and his wife.

She sat in the back of the car and took deep breaths to calm herself down.

There was nothing to be nervous of. All she had to do was hold the fort until Jake arrived. If she kept the conversation general she would be fine.

★ ★ ★

When she arrived at the restaurant, she was shown straight to a table at a window that had a beautiful view of the harbour, and had just sat down when the clients arrived.

'Señor and Señora Tabaras, Señorita McKenzie,' the waiter announced as he pulled out a seat first for Mrs Tabaras and then her husband.

Smiling brightly, Kendall greeted them in Spanish, explaining that Jake had been delayed and would join them shortly. Then she ordered drinks and chattered away to them as best she could. They were a nice couple and were careful not to rattle away too fast — as many Spaniards did — so Kendall could easily follow the conversation. And it wasn't long before Jake arrived, full of apologies for being late.

As the meal progressed, he discussed business with Claude while Kendall chatted to Elina Tabaras. But all the time, she was aware of him beside her, his face giving away nothing of what had happened earlier that evening and his whole manner charming, professional and completely sincere.

Claude obviously thought so, too, because by the time the meal was over, Jake had the contract he wanted.

'That went well,' Kendall said as they were driven back to the hotel.

'Have you managed to get the business back on track again now? You've landed three contracts since we've been here, to my knowledge.'

He looked at her and smiled. 'Yes, I have, thanks to you. I could never have pulled off that deal without your help.'

'I didn't do anything. You did all the negotiating.'

'You sorted my scribbled notes into a well-presented contract and dealt very efficiently with Claude and his wife in my absence. They looked as if they were having a very good time when I arrived.'

'I must admit I wondered if my Spanish would rise to the occasion,' she confessed. 'I'm just glad I didn't let you down.'

Jake reached out and placed his hand over hers, sending goosebumps up her arm. 'I don't think you would ever knowingly let anyone down, Kendall,' he said softly.

She gazed into his eyes and felt herself melting. Mesmerised, she watched as his face came closer and closer until his lips tenderly brushed hers. Then suddenly he was kissing her hungrily and she was returning his kiss with a passion she hadn't known she possessed, pressing herself closer to him, entwining her arms around his neck and acting like she'd been waiting all her life for him, and now that she had him she was never going to let him go.

There was a cough from the front of the car.

'We're here now, sir.'

Kendall broke free in horror and straightened her dress, her cheeks flushing crimson. Necking in the back of the car like a couple of teenagers!

How embarrassing!

'Thank you, Carlos.' Jake straightened his tie and grinned ruefully at her. 'You do seem to have this effect of making me want to kiss you,' he whispered.

'Really? I wasn't aware that I'd forced myself upon you,' she replied, tartly.

'I wasn't implying that you had. I was just remarking that I seem to find you irresistible.' He was amused. 'But maybe I should make sure we're somewhere private before I kiss you again. Darn!'

She glanced around to see Leticia coming towards them, and felt as though a cold flannel had been thrown over her.

'I'm sorry, but there's something I have to deal with,' he told her. 'I'll have to leave you to see yourself to your room.'

'I think I can manage that,' she retorted sharply. 'I'm a big girl now.'

He threw her a searching glance. 'Kendall . . . '

But she was already walking way.

* * *

She made herself a cup of hot chocolate in her room and sat down, sipping it, mulling over what had happened in the limousine. It was ridiculous and down-right embarrassing. Fancy necking in the back of the car like that!

Forget it, the guy will be out of your hair soon, she told herself. Think about something else. Think about your future. She didn't need Jake.

She had a quick shower, changed into her nightie, then climbed into bed

141

to look over the notes she'd made about the finca.

As she started reading through them, excitement welled up in her at the thought of the new life that lay ahead of her.

Then, suddenly — 'Kendall. It's Jake. Are you awake?'

Jake! What was he doing outside her door? And more to the point, how could she let him see her with no make-up, her hair tousled, and wearing her nightie?

'Kendall. I need to speak to you,' he insisted.

She slid out of bed, grabbed her silk wrap off the chair and tied it around herself. She'd have to speak to him. And did it matter what she looked like? It wasn't as if she could ever match up to luscious Leticia anyway. Neither would she ever want to.

She opened the door slightly and peered out.

'I thought you were having a drink with Miss Sinclair,' she said, trying to sound as if she wasn't the slightest bit bothered that he'd kissed her and then gone straight to another woman's arms.

He looked tired and drawn. A frown was etched across his forehead and there was a pained look in his eyes as if he'd just received a blow.

'I've found out who's been betraying us. I saw your light on, guessed you were still up and thought you might like to know.'

Whoever the culprit was, the discovery had really shaken him, she realised. It must have been a really trusted member of staff.

For a moment she hesitated — should she let him in when she was in her nightwear? It didn't seem right. Then again, he seemed so distressed.

'I'm sorry, I shouldn't have come so late. I should have realised you'd be ready for bed,' he told her. 'I'll talk to you in the morning.'

As he turned away her heart won over her head. 'No, it's fine. I was just going through some paperwork. Come in, if you'll excuse my attire,' she said flippantly.

She opened the door wider and stepped to the side to allow him to pass by, then shut the door behind him.

He strode over to a chair and sat down wearily.

'Was it the person you suspected?' she asked, taking the seat opposite him and silently thanking Emma for swapping those naff nightshirts for the white nightie and glamorous, matching silk wrap.

He nodded. 'Luis, our manager has recently acquired a new girlfriend and this girlfriend just happens to be a cousin of the director of Clavero's.'

'So the information wasn't deliberately leaked?' she asked, relieved.

'Not deliberately on the part of the manager. He was just careless, trying to impress his beautiful, new girlfriend. But the woman is a different matter entirely. I'm afraid it was deliberate on her part.'

'You mean she befriended him just to

get the information from him?'

'Oh, yes, she knew exactly what she was doing and what effect it would have on my business.'

'What an underhand thing to do!'

'It was more than underhand. It was downright malicious. This woman knew exactly what she was doing and was motivated out of pure spite.' Jake looked her straight in the eye. 'It was Leticia, Kendall. She's the one who's been scheming to ruin my business.'

She stared at him, stunned. Leticia! She could hardly believe it. His own girlfriend was not only two-timing him but destroying his business as well!

'Oh, Jake, how awful!' she whispered, seeing the hurt in his eyes and wanting to kiss it away. 'But why would she do that?'

'Because she doesn't like being spurned.' He ran his fingers distractedly through his hair. 'Leticia and I have been dating for a while, but it was nothing serious. She knew the score.'

'It was just for fun.' The words were

out before she could stop them.

He looked at her levelly. 'We're both adults,' he said curtly. 'We both knew there was nothing lasting between us.'

She remembered how Leticia had looked at Jake and how she had clung possessively to his arm.

'But Leticia wanted more than fun from you,' Kendall said to him now.

'Yes, she wouldn't take 'no' for an answer. She kept turning up at the office, she even followed me here . . . ' His voice tailed off.

'So because you didn't want her she decided to teach you a lesson?'

'She told me it was all my own fault. That I had spurned her and hurt her.' He looked at Kendall. 'But I liked her, respected her, and would never have deliberately hurt her.'

Images of Jake and Leticia in each other's arms, kissing each other, embracing, went round and round in her mind.

Stop it! she told herself.

'What are you going to do? Will you sack Luis?'

'I'll think about it overnight before I decide what action to take. I know how persuasive Leticia can be. The poor man never had a chance.'

He stood up.

'Well, I'll go now. I've kept you up late enough. I just wanted to let you know that the problem is solved and that we'll be going home as soon as I can book us a flight.'

She followed him to the door. 'Jake . . . '

He turned to face her. 'Yes?'

'I'm so sorry,' she said softly. 'What Leticia did was despicable.'

'It certainly was.' His voice was grim. 'But she will regret it.'

He walked out of the door, pulling it shut behind him.

She will regret it. The way he'd said the words chilled her. He would have his revenge. Leticia was a society animal and by the time Jake had spread the word around about her underhand dealings, Kendall doubted if she would get invited to many parties or social occasions — at least not amongst the high society set she aspired to belong to.

Jake Newman was definitely not the sort of man you crossed lightly.

A Date With Jake

To her relief, Jake seemed in a better mood the next morning. 'How would you like to stay on here for the weekend instead of flying home today?' he asked as they ate breakfast. 'We've both worked hard and deserve some relaxation. If you like, we could do a bit of sightseeing together?'

Kendall took another sip of her orange juice as she considered his offer. He seemed to have regained his good humour but why did he want her to spend the weekend with him? Was he looking for a replacement now that Leticia was out of the picture? She had to face it, there was definitely an attraction between them and if she wasn't careful she could end up getting in deeper than she wanted. Maybe it would be best to go home.

'Or maybe Pete's expecting you

back?' he asked.

'Pete?' She looked at him question-ingly. 'What's Pete got to do with anything?'

'Well, aren't you two an item?'

She decided that it was time to clarify the situation. 'No, we aren't,' she said. 'What made you think that?'

He looked a bit embarrassed. 'I saw him leaving your apartment early on Tuesday morning. And you had lunch with him the day before, remember?'

So he thought she was going out with Pete, yet he'd still kissed her. Did that mean he thought she was cheap or that he couldn't resist her?

'Pete came round on Monday night to look at some of my jewellery. He wants me to make a bracelet for his mum's birthday,' she explained. 'He left his coat behind when he took Emma home, so he had to come round early for it the next morning before I left for Spain.'

His heart soared. She wasn't going out with Pete! She wasn't involved with anyone. There was nothing stopping him from asking her to go out with him.

Nothing except the fact that she was his employee. Only for a couple more weeks, though. They could just be friends for now, then perhaps once she'd stopped working for him they could take their friendship further. Why not go with the flow for now and just enjoy her company?

'You make jewellery?' he asked.

He looked at the pendant she was wearing. It was expertly crafted and very unusual. In fact, she always wore unusual jewellery.

'Did you make that necklace?'

'Yes. I only ever wear my own jewellery.'

'You mean you made that lovely ethnic bracelet you wore last night? And the crystal necklace the night before?'

He shouldn't sound so surprised, as if he thought she wasn't capable of it, he chided himself.

She nodded. 'Yes, every piece of

jewellery I wear, I've made myself.'

He reached out and lifted up the pendant. 'It's beautiful,' he said.

And so was she.

'You're very talented.'

She smiled. 'Thank you.'

Why did a smile from her seem like a gift from the Gods?

For a moment, the silence stretched taut between them as he stroked the pendant, his eyes on her face, and a hot wave of desire rushed through him, the sheer force of it taking his breath away.

He released the pendant and leaned back in his chair, trying to act composed as he gathered together his shattered senses.

'So, what do you say? Would you like to spend a couple of days relaxing in Spain?' he asked when he finally trusted himself to speak calmly.

'There's a flight leaving on Sunday evening.'

'Sounds good to me,' she agreed.

He felt his heart flip over. He longed to reach out and touch her, stroke her face, kiss her lips, hold her in his arms and never let her go.

He fought to keep his voice level. 'Good. I'll arrange the return flights, and for us to stay on at the hotel for an extra couple of days. Now, we'd better get back to work. I'll have to call a meeting to let everyone know what's happened. The place has been buzzing with gossip and speculation since we arrived and it's about time I put a stop to the rumours and let everyone know that things are back to normal again.'

'Have you decided what you're going to do about Luis?' she asked, her eyes full of genuine concern.

'I've decided to give him another chance. I'm sure that he had no idea what Leticia was up to. But I'm issuing him with a written warning. One more careless mistake like that and he's out.'

The smile she gave him was reward enough.

'That's very decent of you.'

'I like to think that I'm a good judge of character.' He leaned back, resting his arms on the table and linking his long fingers together. 'You might think that I offered you this job on an impulse, but I knew you would be good at it.'

She raised her eyebrows questioningly. 'I don't see how you could tell anything about me from the brief time you'd known me apart from the fact that I wasn't very good at steering pushchairs.'

He grinned at her. 'It doesn't take me long to weigh up a person. Do you think I would have given you my credit card if I hadn't known I could trust you?'

It was true, he realised; as soon as he'd seen her he had known he could trust her.

She was smiling again, a teasing smile this time that he longed to kiss away.

'Why, thank you, kind sir,' she quipped. 'But if I hadn't sensed I could trust you then I wouldn't have left baby Sophie with you, credit card or no credit card.'

'I know that.'

She looked at him, her emerald eyes holding his gaze, and it was all he could do to stop himself from leaning over the table and pulling her towards him.

'Come on, we'd better get to work,' he told her. 'I should have all the loose ends at the office tied up by lunch time and then we can have the afternoon off.'

She laughed, a real laugh that revealed her neat white teeth, and crinkled the corners of her eyes.

'You make it sound like we're playing hookey.'

'We deserve to leave early after all the hard work we've done. We've achieved what we came here for, so I think the very least we owe ourselves is an afternoon off and a relaxing weekend. Agreed?'

'I wouldn't dare disagree with the boss,' she told him. 'I'll go along with whatever you want.'

If only she knew that all he wanted was to hold her in his arms!

★　★　★

As soon as they arrived at the office, Jake held a meeting to explain to everyone that the informant had been found and dealt with — without mentioning any names. Then he and Kendall spent the rest of the morning finalising the Tabaras contract and making sure everything was in order.

It was a hectic morning and the effort of forcing herself to concentrate on the letters she was typing, instead of daydreaming about spending the whole weekend with Jake, had given Kendall a splitting headache. She'd had to take two painkillers or she'd never have got through it.

Finally, they had a meeting with Toni to discuss the various contracts and any other outstanding issues.

'I think that ties everything up.' Jake rose from his seat, indicating that the meeting was over.

'Thank you for your assistance in dealing with this matter, Toni. And for contacting me so quickly. Because of your prompt action I've managed to salvage the contracts and there's been no real harm done.'

The other man's face flushed with pride as he stood up to shake Jake's hand. 'It's a pleasure, sir.'

'And I'd appreciate it if you'd leave it to me to mention this to my father,' Jake said as they walked to the door. 'The problem's been solved so I see no need to worry him whilst he's on holiday.'

'Of course.'

'Thank you.'

Toni turned to Kendall. 'It's been a pleasure to meet you, Señorita,' he told her. 'I hope we meet again soon.'

'You never know.' She smiled at him.

Jake took her arm and, as usual, her skin tingled with the contact.

'Kendall and I have decided to extend our stay until Sunday so, if anything crops up that you need to talk to me about, just call me on my mobile,' he told Toni.

Then, keeping a light but firm grip on her arm, he led Kendall out of the room, guiding her down the corridor and through reception.

She noticed the receptionist looking enviously in their direction and knew that Jake holding her like that, almost proprietorially, made it look as if their relationship was more than business.

If it had been anyone else she'd have immediately moved away but with him it felt so right.

She was so happy to walk by his side as he led her out of the building, into the baking sunshine. Then, as if he'd just realised that he was still hanging on to her, he abruptly released his grip and she felt almost bereft.

'So, did you want to visit your parents again this afternoon, or do you fancy coming with me to do a bit of sightseeing?'

They were approaching his BMW.

He took the keys out of his pocket and pressed the remote control.

The doors unlocked with a soft click.

He perched himself on the boot, stretched his oh-so-long legs out in front of him, folded his arms casually and grinned at her. 'What do you think? Could you put up with my company if I promise not to act the boss?'

The prospect of spending an afternoon in this glorious sunshine with Jake was irresistible. So irresistible that common sense told her she should politely decline, but she threw caution to the winds and smiled at him.

'My parents have plans of their own for this weekend, which I don't want to spoil by inviting myself back to Antiquera out of the blue. So, yes, I'd be glad to have your company on a sightseeing expedition. But I'd like to change into something cooler, first.'

She'd dressed in a navy cotton skirt and white top that morning, which had been fine in the air-conditioned office but, out here, with the sun beating down on her, had begun to feel hot and sticky.

'Me, too,' he agreed. 'How about we go back to the hotel, get changed, have a spot of lunch and then set off?'

'Sounds good to me.'

'Let's go then.'

He walked over to the passenger door and opened it for her.

'Your carriage awaits, Señorita.'

'Gracias.'

She followed him and slid herself into the front seat, determined to relax and just enjoy the day.

★　★　★

Back at the hotel, she quickly showered and changed into a lemon seersucker dress with thin shoulder straps.

It finished a couple of inches above her knee, perfect for sightseeing on a sunny afternoon like this.

She surveyed her reflection in the mirror. Her tanned face didn't need any make-up so she just applied a touch of mascara and some pale-pink lipstick.

She didn't want it to look as if she'd made too much effort but she wanted Jake to think she looked good.

She felt nervous and excited at the same time, as if she was going out on her first date.

She'd arranged to meet him in the hotel restaurant for lunch, and when she arrived he was already sitting at the table, sipping a glass of iced water.

He was wearing jeans and white T-shirt that was cut away at the shoulders to reveal powerful, tanned arms, and her tummy did a flip at the sheer sensual magnetism he exuded.

His eyes rested on her as she walked towards him and she saw by the look in them that the attraction was definitely mutual.

'I thought I'd just have salad,' he told her. 'How about you?'

'I'll have the same, thanks.'

She picked up the jug of iced water that was standing in the middle of the table and poured herself a glass, trying to stop her hand from shaking. She had never been so aware of a guy in her life and it both exhilarated her and scared her stiff.

Kendall liked to be in control of her feelings. She had an idea that Jake did too.

★ ★ ★

To her delight, he'd swopped his BMW for an open-topped, dark-green MGB, and they spent a wonderful afternoon driving through the mountains, stopping every so often to wander around the various villages.

He was the perfect companion, friendly and amusing and Kendall thoroughly enjoyed herself.

'Would you like to go shopping for more clothes since we're staying on for a couple of extra days?' Jake asked as they headed back towards Marbella. 'My offer of the use of the business credit card still holds. I can't expect you to be out of pocket just because I've changed our plans.'

'There's no need. I brought a couple of extra outfits with me just in case,' she said. 'But I would like to stop off and buy some beachwear since I didn't bring any with me. Perhaps there are some local shops we can go to? I don't fancy traipsing around a big shopping mall.'

'There are a good range of shops in the next village that we'll come to. I'm sure you'll find something suitable there. They have local pottery that's really unique, too, if you're looking for souvenirs for your friends?'

'That sounds good. I'd like to buy something for Lindsay and Emma. I usually take them back souvenirs from my travels,' she told him.

★　★　★

He was right, the pottery was wonderful. Kendall bought a lovely vase for Emma and a colourful fruit bowl for Lindsay. She also found some hand-made toys for Timmy and Sophie, and a rather expensive white bikini with a brightly coloured sarong for herself.

Jake insisted on buying her a multicoloured beach bag to put her purchases in, as a thank-you for all her hard work over the past few days.

'How do you fancy going to the beach with me tomorrow?' he asked her casually when they returned to the hotel. 'We could have a picnic in a pretty cove I know. It's only about half an hour's drive away and it's a lot nicer than sharing a beach with a crowd of other people.'

She knew exactly what he meant. She hated crowded beaches herself.

'Yes, I'd like that,' she heard herself say. 'What time shall we leave?'

'How about straight after breakfast, then we can spend the morning there?' he suggested. 'And be sure to bring along lots of sun lotion.'

'I'd better buy some more actually,' she told him. 'I wasn't expecting to be sunbathing so I only brought a little bottle with me.'

'No problem. I've got plenty. You can share mine.'

She blotted out the enticing thought of rubbing sun lotion on to Jake's muscular back. 'Thanks.'

'You're welcome,' he said with a grin. 'But the day isn't over yet. How about joining me for dinner at the hotel, then we can go on to La Bella Casa? Toni phoned me to say that he and his wife, Alona, will be there. Apparently there's an excellent show on tonight.'

He mentioned the name of a well-known pop group and told her that they had star billing at the very up-market nightclub.

'I'd love to.' She hesitated. 'The trouble is, I'm not sure that I have anything with me that's suitable to wear to a place like that.'

'Don't worry. Any of the evening dresses you've worn so far will be fine,' he told her.

She had also packed the emerald-green dress she'd worn to Hugh and Tanya's party. Jake had already seen her in it but what did that matter?

'Then I'd love to come,' she agreed. 'What time do you want to meet for dinner?'

'Shall we say eight o'clock? That will give us time for a leisurely meal before we head off for the club.'

'Eight o'clock it is, then.'

That gave her just over an hour to shower and change. It was a good thing she wasn't high maintenance!

★ ★ ★

Jake suppressed a smile as he saw Kendall tucking into her food with evident relish. She was so different to the sort of women he usually went out with; she was so relaxed, so funny and so natural. Most of his dates worried so much about their figures that they barely touched their food, but Kendall — even though she had a stunning figure, which was shown off to perfection in that gorgeous dress — was obviously really enjoying her dinner.

'More wine, Señorita?' asked the young waiter who was hovering around the table.

'Yes, please,' Kendall replied with a smile.

The waiter went to pick up the bottle of wine but it slipped from his grasp, spilling over the tablecloth and into Kendall's lap.

'Lo siento mucho!' he stammered, looking stricken. 'I am so sorry, Señorita! Please forgive me!'

Jake jumped to his feet, seized the cloth from the waiter's hand, dipped it into the water jug and started dabbing at the red stain on Kendall's dress, hoping to stop it from setting.

The poor waiter danced around, wringing his hands and apologising profusely.

'Tranguilo no es ninghun problema,' Kendall reassured him, not seeming the least perturbed as she continued to tell him, in Spanish, not to worry, accidents happen.

Then she thanked Jake, took the wet cloth from him and dabbed at the dress herself.

The manager had seen what had happened and came rushing over to add his apologies and to scold the young waiter.

'I am so sorry, Señorita, he is young and clumsy. Allow me to pay for your dress to be cleaned. And the meal will be on the house, for both of you, Señor,' he said, turning to Jake.

'It's very kind of you, but there's no need,' Kendall told him. 'And please don't punish the waiter — it was an accident.'

'You are most gracious, Señorita.' The manager bowed. 'But I insist you allow us to pay for your dress to be cleaned. It is too beautiful to allow to ruin.'

'Your dress will stain if you don't get it cleaned immediately,' Jake pointed out.

'I know, and I'm afraid this wet cloth isn't doing any good.'

Kendall thanked the manager and accepted his offer, then she turned to the waiter and told him, yet again, not to worry.

The young man smiled and thanked her profusely.

Finally, after extracting a promise that she would hand her dress into reception to be cleaned, the manager and waiter left to attend to the other diners.

'I'd better go and change,' Kendall said, standing up. 'I'm afraid that I might have to give the club a miss. I'm not sure if any of my other outfits are suitable.'

'I'm sure they are. You have excellent taste in clothes.' Jake couldn't imagine her looking less than gorgeous in anything. 'I don't mind what you wear so long as you come.'

Drat, that sounded as if he was desperate for her company!

She flashed him an appreciative smile. 'I'll meet you in reception in ten minutes,' she said.

Yeah, right, thought Jake. He'd never known a woman get changed in ten minutes.

He finished his wine, then left the restaurant and walked over to the reception desk, glancing at his watch. Exactly ten minutes had passed. He might as well have a seat and read the newspaper while he waited.

'Will this be OK to wear to La Bella Casa, do you think?'

He turned around and whistled softly. He'd say it would do! She looked absolutely sensational — the slinky black dress fitted her as if she'd been poured into it, and the black stilettos she was wearing emphasised her long legs.

Her jewellery was incredible too, a chunky silver and garnet necklace with matching earrings.

He reached out to touch the necklace, his hand caressing her skin as he did so. She didn't pull away.

'Did you make this?' he asked. 'It's beautiful. And so is the dress.'

'Thank you. Are you sure it isn't a bit too . . . err . . . clingy?'

Finishing just above her ankle, with a long side slit, the dress certainly was clingy, but it was also very classy and elegant.

'It's absolutely perfect. I'll be the envy of every man there,' Jake told her. And he meant it. Kendall was going to turn heads in that dress and he was delighted that he'd be the one accompanying her.

* * *

He was right, Kendall's appearance certainly attracted lots of attention at the nightclub, yet if she was aware of it she didn't show it and made no attempt to flirt with the various men who asked her to dance, declining every invitation politely.

Jake, however, could barely conceal his annoyance when he saw that she'd been stopped en route to the ladies' room by a smooth-talker who fancied his chances.

Toni and Alona, seemed to find his reaction amusing.

'Tell me, my friend, if you and Kendall are not an item then why are you so furious whenever anyone else pays her attention?' Toni asked, amused.

'Because she's my guest and I don't want her to be pestered like that; it's bad manners,' Jake told him, rising from the table. 'I'll go and rescue her. She must be feeling uncomfortable.'

'She seems to be coping very well to me,' Alona said. 'A woman who looks like Kendall must be used to dealing with unwanted attention.'

She was right, Jake acknowledged. Before he was even halfway across the floor, Kendall had politely disengaged herself from the attentions of the young Spaniard and had disappeared into the cloakroom.

She looked surprised when she came out to found him standing outside the door. 'Are you waiting for me?'

'I noticed a man bothering you as you made your way over here and was worried that you might feel a bit threatened. So I thought I'd escort you back to our table,' he told her defensively.

She laughed, her eyes twinkling. 'That's very kind of you but I'm a big girl now and I've travelled all over the world by myself. I'm perfectly capable of dealing with the odd flirt.'

'Maybe, but you're with me tonight, and you don't have to deal with it,' he said, taking her arm. 'When I take a woman out I like to look after her properly.'

'Goodness, you make it sound like we're dating.' Kendall turned to face him, her eyes challenging.

'Is that such a bad idea?' he heard himself say. 'I like you and I think you like me and we're both free agents?'

Her eyes widened in surprise. 'I'm your secretary,' she reminded him. 'I thought you didn't date staff.'

'You're my temporary secretary and I'm not suggesting we get married! Just that we enjoy each other's company and get to know each other better. What do you say?'

She hesitated for a split second then nodded. 'OK. Why not?'

So much for not getting involved with her, thought Jake, as they walked back to their table, where Toni and Alona were exchanging amused glances.

A Wonderful Weekend

Thank goodness she'd packed a couple of sun dresses, Kendall thought, as she rummaged through her wardrobe next morning and took out a shift dress in a delicate eggshell blue. It was cut in a simple style but the colour suited her.

She decided to wear her swimwear underneath to save the embarrassment of trying to change on the beach, and slipped the sarong into her bag, too, as a cover-up. She added a beach towel and what was left of her sun cream to the bag. Once she'd slipped on a pair of almost flat sandals, she was all set.

She arrived downstairs for breakfast before Jake, and ordered fresh orange juice while she waited for him.

It was unusual for him to be late. Punctuality was one of his strong points.

Perhaps he'd changed his mind and

wasn't going to turn up.

She suddenly realised just how much she'd been looking forward to spending another day in his company.

But, no, he wouldn't stand her up. She'd seen enough of how he handled people these last couple of days to know that if he'd changed his mind he'd come and tell her himself.

Then she caught her breath as she saw him strolling towards her, wearing a pair of washed-out boarding shorts and a tight white vest. She saw that several other female hotel guests were staring admiringly at him and she felt a surge of pride as he sat down beside her.

'Sorry I'm late,' he apologised, flashing her a devastating smile that turned her bones to jelly. 'I had a few calls to answer.'

'Not problems at work, I hope?' she asked, hoping another crisis hadn't come up.

'Just mundane stuff to do with the US office.'

'US office? Does your empire spread all over the world?' She was only half teasing.

'Not quite, but I'm working on it.' His eyes twinkled back at her.

★ ★ ★

After a breakfast of scrambled egg on toast for Kendall and a full fry-up for Jake, they set off in the MGB.

'How many cars do you have?' she asked as they drove off.

'Four. Two over here and two in England,' he told her. 'But this is my favourite.'

'I'm not surprised. It's lovely. Especially on a day like today.'

She loved the feel of the sun on her face and the breeze in her hair as they drove along the motorway.

Before long, Jake turned off along a side-road, then drove down a dirt track which led to the beach.

The cove was breathtaking. Kendall gazed in awe at the golden sand and deep-blue Mediterranean Sea.

'It's beautiful!' she said softly.

'I discovered it a couple of years ago,' Jake told her. 'It's a bit off the beaten track, so it doesn't get as crowded as the tourist beaches, but it's not too far away, either.'

He parked the car and took a picnic basket out of the boot.

'We'll have to walk down a flight of steps,' he told her. 'You might find it difficult in those sandals.'

'No problem.'

She slipped them off and placed them on top of her beach bag.

'Come on, I'll race you,' she said, running ahead.

As she ran towards the steps she heard Jake's footsteps behind her and gave an extra spurt to cover the remaining short distance but, as she reached the top step, her foot slipped on some damp grass and she felt herself hurtle forwards.

Oh heck, I'm going to crash right to the bottom, she thought in panic, but then a strong arm grabbed her, and she fell back against a warm, masculine chest instead. Jake's other arm clasped around her, holding her firmly to him.

'Steady! There's no need to be quite so eager to win!' he said softly.

She could feel his breath on her neck and for a moment she let herself rest against him, enjoying his closeness and the strength of his arms around her.

Then she eased herself out of his embrace.

'Thanks! I thought I was about to get to the bottom rather faster than I'd planned,' she said lightly.

'Don't mention it. I specialise in saving damsels. Now, how about we go down the steps together.' He reached out and took her hand. 'Just to make sure that you get to the bottom in one piece.'

She felt a surge of elation as they walked down the steps, hand in hand.

She was overwhelmed by a feeling of happiness, as if nothing mattered except here and now.

She wanted to be with this man forever.

It was a feeling she'd never experienced before and it was so powerful that she felt in awe of it.

Wake up, Kendall, she told herself. Don't go getting stupid ideas. You're just getting caught up in the romance of the place.

They reached the bottom of the steps and she looked around, taking in her surroundings.

The cove was deserted. The sand stretched out unsullied by human feet in front of her, like a golden blanket. The sea was calm and still, with only the occasional ripple breaking its surface and a few palm trees provided shelter from the sun.

'It's like a tropical island!'

She wondered if he'd ever brought Leticia here, then pushed the thought from her mind. Leticia was the past and she wasn't going to let anything spoil today.

Jake released her hand and walked

over to the nearest palm tree to put down his bag. 'Let's leave our things here,' he suggested. 'It'll provide us with some shade. How about a swim?'

Suddenly aware of how private the beach was, she felt embarrassed at the thought of taking off her sun dress to reveal her skimpy bikini, but Jake had no such inhibitions. He was already pulling off his vest top to reveal a muscular chest.

She turned and quickly slid out of her dress, folded it and put it in her bag.

When she turned around she saw Jake running over the sand to the sea, his long, strong legs striding out effortlessly.

'Hey, come on, slowcoach!' he called to her over his shoulder.

Kendall padded after him across the soft sand. He had his back to her as she joined him in the cool water so she playfully splashed him.

He laughed, then turned and ran towards her through the sea.

With a couple of long strides he was beside her and, before she realised what his intentions were, he'd wound an arm around her waist and had pulled her towards him.

Before she could resist, his mouth came down on hers and he was kissing her passionately, holding her close.

She returned his kisses, winding her arms around his neck and running her hands through his dark curly hair, pulling him closer. The sea lapped gently around their legs as, oblivious to everything, she lost herself in his embrace.

Then, suddenly, he released his hold on her. 'I'm sorry,' he told her seriously. 'For a moment there I forgot that I was a gentleman.'

Tenderly, he took her hand and raised it to his lips for a moment before letting it go. He gave her a wry smile before turning to dive into the water.

As he swam away from her, Kendall shivered, hugging her arms around her. Was she getting in deeper than she could handle?

Jake made no attempt to kiss her again and, although she longed for his touch, she was grateful for his restraint. She was having enough trouble keeping a check on her emotions as it was, and she knew he felt the same.

★ ★ ★

They didn't spend long sunbathing on the beach, choosing to spend the rest of the day sightseeing instead. First, they paid a visit to the market in Puerto Banus, where they bumped into Kendall's parents.

She introduced Jake as her boss, and he behaved impeccably, but she saw the knowing look her mother gave her and knew that the attraction between them hadn't escaped her eagle eye.

Luckily, her parents were meeting friends and couldn't chat for long.

'I'll phone you later, dear,' her mother said as they left.

Kendall groaned. 'Oh no, she'll be wanting to quiz me about you,' she told

Jake. 'I know that look.'

'That 'might this lead to a wedding' look, you mean?' he asked, his voice laced with amusement.

'Something like that,' she admitted ruefully. 'You know how mothers get when you're over twenty-five and you show no sign of settling down. I'm sure yours is the same.'

She saw a dark shadow pass over his face, then he replied. 'My mother died from cancer when I was a child, but I know what you mean. My father is always dropping hints that I should settle down.'

'I'm sorry about your mother.' She reached out and touched his arm. 'It must have been awful for you.'

'It was.'

He looked as if he was going to say something else but instead, he forced a smile that didn't quite reach his eyes. He obviously didn't want to talk about his family so she didn't force the issue.

'There's a shoe stall on the other side of the market. I wonder if we can find a pair of shoes to match the beach bag I bought for you.'

They didn't find shoes to match the beach bag, but Kendall did find a lovely pair of sandals the exact same shade of blue as the dress she was wearing.

Before she could pay for them, Jake took them from her.

'My treat,' he insisted and handed over the money to the stall holder.

'Thank you.' She smiled and immediately put on the new shoes, placing her other sandals in her beach bag.

They had lunch in a restaurant overlooking the harbour, then returned to the car and Jake drove to Fuengirola where they spent the rest of the afternoon.

★   ★   ★

It's been a perfect day, Kendall thought as they drove back to the hotel. She'd enjoyed Jake's company immensely. He was a wonderful companion, good fun and considerate.

'What would you like to do this

evening?' he asked as he pulled into the hotel car park. 'How about a meal at the hotel and a quiet drink?'

He parked the car, switched off the engine and turned to face her. 'Or would you prefer to do something else? Take in a show, perhaps, or visit a club?'

'A meal at the hotel would be lovely,' she said. It would give them a chance to talk some more and to get to know one another better.

'Great. I'll reserve a table. Shall we say about half-past eight?'

'Fine, that'll give me time to shower and change.'

'There's no need to dress up. Let's keep it casual,' he told her. 'Just a relaxing chat and a meal. Deal?'

'Deal,' she agreed.

★ ★ ★

Jake was glad Kendall had chosen to spend the evening in the hotel, just the two of them, rather than going to a club or show.

Towel tied around his waist, he padded barefoot across the carpet to the wardrobe. He selected a dark-blue shirt and some co-ordinating chinos. He wanted the meal to be relaxed, to get to know Kendall better, to find out what made her tick.

You shouldn't be doing this, he told himself as he removed the towel and sprayed himself with expensive cologne. He never mixed business with pleasure. Never dated anyone he worked with. It always meant trouble. Yet, here he was going out with his PA.

Temporary PA, he reminded himself, slipping on his shirt and buttoning it up. That made a difference.

But maybe he should have waited until Joyce had returned to work before he'd asked Kendall out? It would have been the sensible thing to do but he just couldn't seem to be sensible around Kendall.

He called for her as arranged, at half-past eight. She opened the door as soon as he knocked on it, looking effortlessly gorgeous in a simple, red dress that emphasised her slender waist and danced around her hips as she walked.

Her jewellery was simple too, a ruby-red three-drop pendant and matching earrings.

'Have you ever thought of trying to sell your designs?' he asked her after they'd ordered dinner. 'I'm sure one of the established jewellery firms would be interested in them.'

'Maybe, but I don't want someone else making my jewellery. I want to do it all myself, and to market my work under my own label.'

'If that's what you want to do, then why are you travelling the world teaching English?' He looked genuinely interested.

'Two reasons,' she replied. 'One is to save enough money so that I can eventually work full-time at what is at the moment only a hobby. The other is because I find that going to other countries and experiencing different cultures gives me inspiration. I had the idea for this design when I was working in Asia.'

She fingered the ruby-red pendant as she spoke.

'But surely teaching English as a foreign language isn't that well paid? How long do you think it will take you to save the money you need?'

'No, it isn't a well paid job, but the accommodation is usually thrown in too, and I rent out my flat while I'm away which leaves some money to spare.'

She was tempted to tell him about her plans to move to Spain but something held her back.

'How many pieces of jewellery have you got in your range so far?' he asked.

She did a quick calculation as the waiter appeared with their first courses.

She was relieved to see that it was the same waiter that they'd had the night before, so he hadn't been given the sack. He smiled at her and carefully placed a bowl of prawns in front of them.

'About thirty pieces in all,' she replied, as the waiter departed.

'That's quite an impressive collection. Why don't you take it to one of the leading jewellery firms and see if they'll offer you a job and give you your own label? Then you could gain more experience and make contacts before setting up on your own.'

That would make sense, she had to admit, but she wanted to make a go of her jewellery by herself.

'It can be tough setting up your own company, but I understand the appeal. There's nothing like being your own boss.' He picked up the bottle of wine. 'Would you like some more?'

She nodded and swallowed the last of her prawns before asking, 'Do you like being your own boss?'

'I did when I ran my own website design firm,' he told her, topping up her glass. 'I enjoyed the challenge of building it up from scratch, getting my first contract, watching my client base and bank balance steadily grow. It was hard work and long hours, but it was something I, too, was determined to achieve by myself.'

So he hadn't always run EXA Electronics then, she thought, as the waiter came to clear their table, ready for the second course.

'What made you give it up to join your father's business?' she asked.

His face clouded over and his eyes glittered like steel.

'A few years after my mother died, my father married again. But my stepmother was only after his money. She cheated on him numerous times and when he finally divorced her she fleeced him for as much as she could get. The stress proved too much for him, he had a heart attack and the business was on the verge of bankruptcy because he'd neglected it for so long. What else could I do?'

No wonder he hated betrayal. His stepmother had almost destroyed his father and caused him to give up his own dream. Leticia betraying him as

190

she did must have cut him to the core.

She reached out and placed her hand over his.

'I'm sorry.'

His eyes softened and he smiled at her.

'I shouldn't be boring you with all this. Let's talk about what we're going to do tomorrow. Our plane doesn't leave until the evening so we've got all day to fill.'

'How about having another drive around?' she suggested. 'I'd love to see more of the mountain villages. They're so pretty.'

'OK,' he agreed. 'We'll spend the day sightseeing. Bring some strong walking shoes and a hat though; the afternoon sun is really intense.'

'Yes, sir!' She gave him a mock salute and he rewarded her with a devastating grin.

Her heart turned over. What was she getting herself into?

Back To Reality

Anxious not to waste a moment of their last day in Spain, Jake and Kendall set off on their sightseeing trip straight after breakfast.

Heading inland from Malaga, he steered the MGB effortlessly along the rugged tracks through the mountains.

Luckily, Kendall was used to the narrow roads that dipped and curved around hairpin bends, so she could relax and enjoy the wonderful scenery without panicking that they were going to go over the side of the mountain.

Groves of olive and almond trees were scattered everywhere, whilst far below them lay the aquamarine sea, glistening under the sun's rays. It was truly breathtaking.

'Fancy stopping and stretching our legs for a while?' Jake asked as they drove into a Moorish village nestled into the mountainside.

'I'd love to!' She was dying to have a wander around the pretty village with its narrow, cobbled streets and white-washed houses.

He pulled over, parking the sports car off the road, and they both got out.

Immediately a crowd of children ran over and gathered around them, their eyes wide as they stared at the car, chattering excitedly.

Kendall guessed they'd never seen one like it before.

'It's like time has stood still here,' she said, looking around at the simple houses, their wrought-iron balconies filled with colourful flowers, the sun-wrinkled old women, dressed in black, sitting on wooden stools outside their doorways, the old men leading donkeys through the narrow streets, and the crumbled remains of the old Moorish fort at the top of the hill.

The sleepy mountain villages were a sharp contrast to the lively metropoli-tanism of Marbella.

'This is my favourite part of Spain,' Jake told her, 'where life still goes on in the same way that it did hundreds of years ago. The twenty-first century will catch up eventually, of course. More and more people are moving out of the mountain villages and into the towns but, thankfully, it's a slow process. I hate to think of the old Spain disappearing forever.'

'Me, too,' Kendall agreed. 'That's why I love Antiquera where my parents live. It isn't too far from the cities but is remote enough to be out of the hustle and bustle.'

Jake folded his arms and leaned back against the car bonnet, studying her thoughtfully.

'You're not a city girl at heart, then?'

She shook her head. 'Not really. Sure, I love the occasional party and to go to the movies or the theatre now and again, but I prefer to live in the country. And when I go abroad I like to travel off the beaten track and see how the people really live. A city in Spain isn't really so different to a city anywhere else.'

He nodded. 'I know what you mean. I prefer to 'go native' myself.'

For a moment they stood in companionable silence, taking in their surroundings.

Then Jake pressed the remote to lock the car.

'Come on, let's take a walk around.'

'Will the car be OK?' She looked dubiously at the crowd of children around the MGB.

He took a few coins out of his pocket and handed them to one of the older boys, speaking rapidly to him in Spanish, telling him to look after the car until they came back and then he would be given more money.

'Si, Señor. Gracias,' the boy said, smiling eagerly.

'Gracias.'

Jake reached for Kendall's hand and clasped it in his as if it was the most natural thing in the world.

'Come on then, let's go walkabout.'

★　★　★

It had been a fantastic afternoon, Kendall thought as they drove back to the hotel. She hadn't wanted it ever to end. She'd wanted it to last for ever, for her to be always holding Jake's hand as they walked around a picturesque village, or to sit for all eternity beside him in his car, the wind blowing in her hair, chatting and laughing as they drove along the coast road. But, of course, it had to end. They had a plane to catch.

Did he intend to continue seeing her socially once they were back home, she wondered, or would things return to business only?

Well, so what? You're moving to Spain soon, she reminded herself. Joyce would be back soon, her job would be finished, she and Jake would say goodbye and she could come back to Spain to start her new life.

After all, they both wanted the same thing. No commitment. So who was going to get hurt?

You. A little voice whispered in her mind. She ignored it. How could she get hurt? All she felt for Jake was infatuation. OK, maybe infatuation wasn't quite the right word for it but it was no big deal. She could handle it.

★   ★   ★

Jake turned into the hotel car park and reversed into a parking space. 'We've got an hour before we need to set off for the airport,' he said. 'I've got some last minute calls to make so I'll leave you to pack and I'll meet you in the lobby at quarter-past five. Is that OK?'

'That's perfect.'

That would give her time to have a shower and to phone her parents. As she'd promised, her mother had called her the previous evening, delighted to hear that she was staying on for the weekend and asking her to pop over with Jake to visit them, but Kendall had made an excuse. Much as she'd like to see her parents again before she flew back to the UK, she didn't want her relationship with Jake open to their scrutiny.

And she didn't want her parents mentioning anything about the finca she was buying. She'd tell Jake about it when it was all sorted out; it was pointless mentioning it until then.

In case you change your mind and want to stay close to him.

She pushed the niggling thought aside. Of course she wouldn't change her mind. This was her big opportunity. There was no way she'd give it up for a man.

* * *

To her disappointment, Jake was preoccupied with paperwork on the flight home.

'Anything I can help with?' she offered, but he shook his head.

'Just a few problems with the US office,' he told her. 'The manager over there faxed some figures to the hotel. It's nothing I can't sort out myself. I'll phone him later tonight and discuss things.'

So she had to content herself with reading a book while he sat in silence beside her, scribbling away at his notes.

The closeness they had shared in Spain seemed years ago rather than just a couple of hours.

I guess that answers my question as to where I stand now we're going home, she thought ruefully. It's back to business. Well, that was fine by her.

She'd only be working with him for a couple more weeks anyway.

Even so, she had to suppress a sigh as the plane landed. It had been a heavenly weekend and she didn't want to return to normality — but she wanted to spend more time with the charming, carefree Jake that she'd spent the last couple of days with, not this distant, preoccupied businessman who was sitting beside her.

Get a grip, she told herself sternly.

You've only been sightseeing together. It's hardly a big romance, is it?

They collected their luggage and went out to where Jake's chauffeur was waiting for them.

'I hope you don't mind if we drop you off at your place and I carry on straight home myself?' he asked. 'I've got some things to sort out.'

'Of course not,' Kendall told him. 'I've got things to sort out myself and I could do with an early night before work tomorrow. It's been an enjoyable but exhausting weekend.'

His eyes met hers, dancing with amusement, and to her annoyance, she felt her face glow pink.

He put out his hand to cover hers as he sat beside her.

'How do you fancy going to the theatre on Monday night? I've got two tickets for a musical.'

Two tickets? She wondered who he'd been planning to take, originally.

Her cheeks had cooled down by now, so she turned to face him.

'Sounds good. I love musicals. Which one is it?'

He named the latest show by an award-winning composer, then leaned over to kissing her cheek. 'We can go for a meal, afterwards,' he said.

She guessed that meant they were still 'dating'. For the time being, anyway.

*   *   *

Jake was already in his office and speaking on the phone when Kendall arrived on Monday morning. He smiled at her and pointed towards the coffee machine. She nodded, walked over and switched it on, then took off her jacket. She needed an intake of caffeine herself or she'd never get through the day.

She hadn't slept well the previous night, despite being so exhausted. She'd kept waking up thinking of Jake — nothing new there, he'd played havoc with her head since she'd met him — so finally she'd got up,

201

showered, had a bowl of cereal and decided to go into the office early, knowing that as they'd been away for four days there was bound to be a lot of work to catch up with.

From the look of the paperwork spread out over his desk, Jake had arrived early at the office too.

She hoped it was because thinking of her had disturbed *his* sleep.

She was just pouring the coffee when, his phone call finished, he came to join her.

'You're in early,' he said, kissing the nape of her neck.

Shivers ran down her back and her arms, almost making her drop the coffee pot.

'Sorry, did I startle you?'

She heard the smile in his voice as, her hand still trembling, she put the pot down.

Before she could answer, he spun her round and kissed her thoroughly on the mouth.

'Should we be doing this?' she asked.

'Don't you have a rule about not fraternising with the staff?'

'Is that what you call this?' He pulled her to him as he kissed her again. 'Fraternising?'

'I guess since I'm only temporary staff, it doesn't really matter,' she said, wrapping her arms around his neck.

He responded with passion and she returned the kiss ardently. Then he reluctantly pulled away, smiling rue-fully.

'Maybe we ought to have that coffee?'

She picked up the coffee pot, willing her hands not to shake, and poured it out.

'How would you like to be my PA permanently?' he asked her, picking up his cup, his eyes never leaving her face.

Kendall stared at him. 'Are you serious? What about Joyce? Surely you're not sacking her?'

She couldn't believe that Jake would consider firing his loyal secretary just because he was going out with her temporary replacement. No, he wouldn't. He wasn't that kind of guy. Was he?

He took a sip of his coffee, then put the cup down on its saucer.

'That was Joyce who was on the phone when you came in. She isn't coming back to work. She's handed in her notice.'

'Why? Isn't her leg getting better?'

'Her leg is healing fine but she's been helping her husband with his paper-work while she's been off sick — he's a self-employed plumber — and appar-ently she's enjoyed it so much she's decided to quit her job and be his secretary instead of mine!'

What should she do? She was tempted to accept his offer. Working permanently for Jake was certainly appealing. More than appealing. Her heart was screaming at her to say yes. But her head was asking her what she would do when he tired of her? Tanya had told her of Jake's reputation for casual relationships.

And she'd have to give up the chance

of living her dream.

'You don't look very enthusiastic.' He was looking at her intently.

'What's the problem? Are you planning on going to work abroad again?'

'Sort of.'

Just tell him, Kendy. As if he'll care! You're only a passing distraction.

She met his gaze.

'I'm moving to Spain. I went to see a finca when I was over there, not far from where my parents live, and I've made an offer for it.'

The silence hung between them as he stared at her, his face expressionless.

She watched him. Waited for him to say something.

Tell me you don't want me to go.

He finished his drink then got up, walked over to the coffee machine and poured himself another cup.

'Would you like one?' he asked, half turning towards her.

She shook her head wordlessly. What was he thinking? Didn't he care that she was going away?

He seemed to take his time stirring the coffee as he walked back over to her, then took a sip before replying.

'So you had decided this before last weekend?' he asked, his voice even.

Change that to — *before we kissed, went out together, agreed to date.*

'Yes,' she told him. 'Why? Does it matter?'

That's it, Kendy, throw the ball in his court. See if he's bothered.

Ignoring her question, he perched himself on the end of her desk, folded his arms casually and scrutinised her. She met his gorgeous brown eyes levelly, her chin tilted defiantly.

'What do you know about this property?' he asked. 'Spanish law is quite different from ours, you know, and many people have fallen in love with a house while on holiday, bought it, and later regretted it.'

So that was it! He didn't think she was capable of making such a decision all by herself. How patronising! And here was she thinking he was bothered about her going away. How stupid of her; after all, he'd made it clear he wasn't into commitment so this probably suited him perfectly. In a couple of weeks he'd have tired of her anyway.

Then why had he offered her Joyce's job?

To save him the bother of getting another secretary, of course. Why else?

'I'm well aware of how the Spanish property system works,' she told him coolly. 'I've contacted a lawyer to deal with the legal side of things and will be having a survey done.'

He nodded. 'Good, but this seems to be rather a spur of the moment decision. I wasn't aware you had any plans to move to Spain.'

'I haven't really known you long enough to discuss my plans for the future, have I?' she retorted.

'Point taken,' he said curtly. 'When exactly are you planning on leaving?'

'Well, I thought I was only here for a couple of weeks, anyway, remember?' she pointed out. 'It will take at least six weeks for all the paperwork to go through in Spain, so I can stay on until then, if you like. To give you time to find a replacement for Joyce.'

'Thank you. I'd appreciate that. Perhaps you could contact a couple of recruitment agencies this morning and arrange interviews for as soon as possible.'

He stood up.

'Now, I'd better get some work done.'

So that was it. No protest.

What did you expect, Kendy? For him to beg you to stay? To say that he can't live without you?

She smiled sweetly at him.

'Of course. I'll get on to the agencies as soon as they open.' She glanced at her watch. 'Which will be in five minutes time.'

Just then the door opened and Steve Nicholson, EXA's general manager, came in.

'Morning, Jake,' he said breezily. 'I hear your mission to Marbella was a resounding success.'

'If you mean that we managed to save the contracts then, yes, you heard right,' Jake replied. 'Come into my office and I'll tell you all about it, then you can fill me in on what's been happening here.'

Well, at least she now knew where she stood with him, Kendall thought, as the two men disappeared into Jake's office. She'd been a casual fling. She was surprised how much that hurt her.

* * *

Jake found it hard to concentrate that day. He couldn't get it out of his mind that Kendall was moving to Spain and, more to the point, that she hadn't even thought it necessary to tell him until he'd offered her a permanent job. Had she intended to tell him at all, he wondered, or would she have just walked out of his life without a backward glance?

He'd hoped that he'd meant more to her than that.

Why? What exactly is there between

the two of you other than mutual physical attraction, he asked himself.

He stood up and paced around the office, his hands in his pockets.

Something about Kendall got right under his skin, like an itch he couldn't scratch. She was funny, honest, kind. He knew their relationship wouldn't have lasted long but he'd thought they'd have more than a couple of weeks together.

I wish we'd had forever.

Whoa! Where did that come from? He didn't do 'forever'. Not with her. Not with anyone. Maybe it was a good thing she was going away after all. Maybe he should cancel their date for that evening and keep their relationship strictly business.

He sat down in his chair and pressed the intercom.

'Can you come into my office for a minute please, Kendall?'

I'll just tell her something's come up and I can't make tonight, he thought, watching through the glass partition as she got up from her desk and walked over to his office, her skirt sashaying around her legs.

'Yes?' she asked, coming in and standing by the door, her cheeks slightly pink.

'About tonight . . . '

'You want to cancel?'

The challenge in her eyes seemed to mock him.

It irked him that she was well aware of what he'd been thinking.

'Not at all. Unless you want to?' He threw the challenge back at her.

She lifted up her head and tossed back her hair. 'Of course not.'

'Then I'll pick you up this evening as planned?'

'That'll be fine.'

So much for keeping his distance, he thought wryly. But if Kendall McKenzie could play it cool and detached, so could he.

Property Problems

It was like the weekend had never happened, Kendall thought when she got home from the theatre, kicked off her shoes and sank down on to the sofa.

All evening, Jake had been friendly, considerate . . . and the perfect gentleman. The only physical contact between them had been when he'd placed his hand on her back to guide her through the crowd in the foyer — an action which had made her want to drag him into the nearest dark corner and kiss him senseless. He hadn't even kissed her goodnight.

She shut her eyes and thought of how well they'd got on in Spain, and she couldn't believe he'd gone off her just like that.

Then she remembered how his eyes had lit up when she'd arrived at the office that morning; how he'd kissed her so passionately.

She shook her head. No, he hadn't gone off her.

Another image flashed across her mind; the look on his face when she'd told him she was going to live in Spain.

Of course, what a fool she was. That's why he'd turned cool towards her.

But why would her move to Spain cause Jake to lose interest? He wasn't looking for a long-term relationship so it shouldn't make any difference to him. Maybe he just liked to be the one to call the shots and say when a relationship was finished.

The ringing of the phone interrupted her thoughts. The cordless handset was on the coffee table by the sofa where she'd left it after talking to Lindsay earlier that evening and she reached out, picked it up and switched it on. 'Hello? Kendall McKenzie speaking.'

'Hi, Kendy, it's Pete. I was wondering when my mum's bracelet will be ready?'

Heck, she'd forgotten all about Pete's mum's bracelet!

'Pete, I'm so sorry! I didn't get back from Spain until yesterday, but I will start on it this week, I promise.'

'OK, no problem. It's still a couple of weeks before her birthday, anyway.' She heard someone murmur in the background, then Pete asked, 'Emma wants to know if you enjoyed your trip to Spain?'

She smiled. So Emma was with him. She had a feeling those two were well-suited to each other.

'Tell her everything went OK.'

She knew that Emma wouldn't be satisfied with that answer and next thing her friend's voice came on the line. 'I want to know about you and Jake. How did you get on?'

Kendall thought about the weekend. Laughing with Jake, kissing him, feeling his arms around her.

'We got on very well, thank you.'

'And?'

'And what?'

'And didn't he try to kiss you or anything?'

Kendall hesitated.

'I knew it!' Emma squealed. 'Come on, tell me! What happened between you and him?'

'Nothing,' Kendall said flatly. 'But I have got something to tell you. I'm moving to Spain. I'm going to buy a house over there.'

'You're what?' Emma's voice rose a pitch. 'You're moving to Spain? But what about you and Jake.'

'There is no me and Jake.'

'Does he know you're going to Spain?'

Kendall sighed. Emma was like a dog with a bone once she got an idea into her head.

Ten minutes later, she finally put down the phone after promising to meet Emma after work the next day to fill her in with all the details.

★   ★   ★

Jake turned off the shower and reached for a towel. Kendall had looked stunning that evening in a deep-blue dress.

As they'd walked into the theatre he'd felt proud to be with her, wanted to hold her in his arms and tell everyone she was his.

Except she wasn't his, was she? She'd been so swept off her feet by him that she'd decided to go and live abroad, which didn't do his ego any good.

He grimaced wryly as he rubbed himself dry with the towel. He was used to women clinging like a limpet to his arm, all starry-eyed. And here was Kendall calmly telling him that she was leaving the country in a few weeks' time without so much as a backward glance. And she'd only told him because she'd felt she had to, because he'd offered to make her job permanent.

He wondered just when she *had* been planning to tell him. As she left for the airport, perhaps?

Darn, he couldn't get her out of his

mind. He could see her, smell her perfume, hear her laugh. How he'd managed to get through the evening without kissing her he'd never know.

He glanced over at the phone and the longing to hear her voice engulfed him but he wasn't going to call her. Definitely not.

She answered the phone on the sixth ring.

'Yes?' She sounded sleepy.

'Kendall?'

'Jake?' Her tone was instantly alert. 'What is it? What's happened?'

He glanced at the clock. It was half-past eleven, a bit late for a social call.

'Sorry to disturb you, I thought you'd still be up.'

'I've only just gone to bed. Is there something wrong?'

No. I just wanted to hear your voice.

'No, it's just I meant to ask you if you could come in a bit earlier tomorrow. I need to run through some figures with you for a new contract before my meeting at ten o'clock. Could you make it for eight-thirty again?'

He could quite easily do the figures himself, but it was the only excuse for calling her that he could think up on the spur of the moment.

'Yes, of course, I will. Goodnight, then.'

He reluctantly put down the phone. Get yourself together, Jake, he told himself. You don't need the hassle. Let her go.

*   *   *

'OK,' Emma said in the pub the next evening, as she and Kendall carried their drinks — white wine and lemonade for Kendall, wine and soda for Emma — over to a table. 'I want all the juicy details.'

'Really, Emma.' Kendall raised an eyebrow teasingly. 'I told you it was a business trip.'

'Then why did you stay over there for the weekend instead of coming home on Friday, like you'd planned?'

'Jake suggested we stay over and do a bit of sightseeing.' Kendall picked up the menu and made a great play of reading it. 'What do you fancy to eat?'

'Never mind that.' Emma took the menu from her. 'Look me in the eyes and tell me that you haven't fallen for him.'

Kendall felt her cheeks turn red.

'I knew it!' Emma was triumphant. 'Anyone at Tanya and Hugh's party could see that you two were interested in each other. But what went wrong? Why are you moving to Spain?'

'Nothing went wrong.'

Memories of Jake kissing her and holding her in his arms flitted across her mind. It all went so right, she thought.

'I'm going because I've found a lovely little finca within my price range with a workshop where I can make my jewellery. It's what I've wanted for ages, Emma. You know that. I can't let this opportunity go by.'

'I wouldn't have thought you could let a guy like Jake go by,' Emma told her. 'He's gorgeous and, more to the point, you're mad about him.'

'I am not!'

'You are and you know it.' Emma looked at her speculatively. 'That's why you're moving to Spain, isn't it? You're running scared because for the first time in your life you've found a guy you really care about.'

Kendall bit her lip as the truth of Emma's words hit home. She was right.

She *was* scared of her feelings for Jake.

'Maybe,' she agreed reluctantly. 'But he doesn't care about me or he'd ask me to stay.'

'He cares about you, all right. Anyone could see the spark between the pair of you. But he won't ask you to stay because he's like you. Frightened of commitment. He's running scared too.'

'OK. I admit that we're attracted to each other. But I'm not messing up my life for physical attraction. I've got a chance to follow my dream and I'm going for it.'

'Even if it means breaking your heart?' Emma asked.

'Don't be so melodramatic,' Kendall told her. 'Jake's a really good-looking guy and he's great company, but I'm not in love with him.'

'Aren't you?' Emma raised an eyebrow. 'Then why are you in such a hurry to get away from him?'

* * *

Emma's words played on Kendall's mind all evening but it wasn't until she walked into the office the next morning, and her heart leapt at the sight of Jake sitting at his desk working, that she realised that Emma was right. She was in love with him.

The realisation shocked her so much that she couldn't move. She stood in the doorway of her office, staring at him blankly, whilst the words, '*I love him*', spun round and round in her mind.

As if sensing her presence he looked up and smiled at her.

Almost as if she was in a dream, she watched him get up from his desk, walk out of his office and over to her.

'Are you all right, Kendall?' he asked softly.

The concern in his eyes shook her. Was Emma right about him, too? Did he love her?

She took a deep breath and forced herself to smile casually back at him.

'I'm fine thanks, just a bit groggy. I met Emma after work last night and we stayed up late, chatting.'

'Would you like a coffee before we start the paperwork?' he asked her.

'You know my weakness for caffeine,' she quipped.

As she watched him walk over to the coffee machine she was so aware of him, of her feelings for him, that she felt suffocated and she could hardly breathe.

'Do you mind if I open a window?' she asked.

'Feel free.' He came back with two

cups of coffee and handed her one. 'Did you contact the employment agencies yesterday and arrange interviews for a replacement secretary?'

'Yes. I've got a few interviews booked for later this week. I've marked them in your diary. I presumed you'd want to do the interviews yourself?'

'Yes, I would.' His eyes met hers. 'Now, if you come through to my office, we'll get on with some work.'

He turned and walked away, leaving her to follow him.

Well, Emma wasn't completely right, Kendall thought dismally. She might be in love with Jake but he wasn't in love with her. If he was then he wouldn't be so casual about her leaving to live in another country. He'd be begging her to stay.

He gestured for her to sit down in the chair on the other side of his desk then passed her a file.

'Here are all the notes and a draft document. I've made a few alterations to our standard contract, as you can see. Read it through and let me know what you think.'

She glanced at the name on the cover of the file.

'You're working with Morgan D'Arcy? The jewellers?'

'Yes, Stella Morgan's a friend of mine. They're looking to update all their computers and want the latest software, so Stella's asked me to give them a quote.'

That brought her down to earth with a bang, she thought. Why on earth would a high-flying millionaire businessman like Jake be in love with someone like her when he could have his pick of all the elegant, beautiful and much more socially-elevated women — like Stella Morgan — who flitted around his high-society world.

Get real, she told herself. Men like Jake look on women like you as a pleasant distraction, not as potential wives.

*   *   *

224

Jake left for his business meeting at half-past ten and Kendall didn't see him for the rest of the day.

She was relieved, because now she'd realised that she loved him, the less she saw of him the better.

She so afraid that she'd do something that would give her true feelings away, and there was no way she wanted to suffer the cringing embarrassment of Jake discovering that she'd fallen for him.

When had it happened? she wondered.

She cast her mind back to the events of the past couple of weeks, trying to identify the moment.

Maybe it had been right at the beginning, as soon as she'd set eyes on him in the department store. He'd certainly made her pulse race and her senses tingle. She'd been so aware of him from that very first moment. Could it have been love at first sight?

No. That sort of stuff only happened in romantic novels. Maybe it had been physical attraction at first sight and somehow that had turned to love.

She didn't know. But she couldn't deny her feelings. She might not want to be in love with him but she was. Fact.

The question was, what was she going to do about it? It was obvious that he didn't love her. Not that she expected him to. Or wanted him to. Love was a complication that she didn't need. She'd seen what it had done to her friends and she had no intention of letting it ruin her life.

No, the best thing was to have as little to do with him as possible. In a couple of weeks time she would be in Spain and would probably never see him again. Then this stupid 'love' that she felt would go away and she could get on with her life. It was the only sensible thing to do.

To her irritation she kept glancing at the door, hoping to see his tall, athletic figure coming through it, and she grabbed the phone every time it rang, hoping to hear his voice on the other end of the line.

She tried to stop doing these things but she couldn't help herself. Just when she thought she'd got her emotions under control, she'd catch herself once more, waiting and watching for a sign of his return.

She'd got it bad. But she could beat this thing. It was just a matter of mind over heart. She'd got to keep busy and not give herself time to think.

In fact, she kept so busy that she not only typed up all the notes that Jake had left for her, but reorganised the entire filing system as well.

★   ★   ★

After work she went late-night shopping, delaying her return to her flat to put off the moment when she'd have to stop, sit down and think, but when she finally arrived home at eight o'clock, exhausted, she spotted a silver BMW parked outside her block and knew instantly that it was his.

He sure liked to ring the changes with his cars, she thought, her heart flipping as the driver's door opened and Jake got out and walked over to wait while she parked her battered, old Fiesta.

'Where have you been?' he demanded, reaching down to drag open the driver's door. 'I've been waiting here for you for over an hour.'

'Really?' She stood on the pavement, smoothing down her skirt and glaring at him. 'Well, I do apologise, but perhaps you could let me know next time you decide to drop by. There's this modern device called a mobile phone, you know?' Her voice dripped with sarcasm.

'I know. I tried to call you but you didn't have a signal. I've left you two messages.'

She opened the boot and reached for her shopping bags but he got there before her.

'I guess you were too busy shopping

to check your phone.'

'Yes, I was.'

She closed the boot, pressed the remote to lock the car, and turned towards him. 'Why did you want to see me? Didn't everything go well at the meeting today?'

'The meeting went fine. But I didn't have a chance to get back to the office today so I couldn't arrange anything with you for tonight. I thought maybe you might want to go out to eat?'

Her heart sang. But the more she saw of him the more she was going to get hurt.

'I'm sorry, but I'm too busy tonight. I'm still trying to catch up with household chores after the few days I've been away.'

She guessed that a bigshot like him would have a housekeeper and wouldn't realise what it was like for lesser mortals like herself.

'Of course. Well, I'll settle for a coffee and a take-away pizza,' he said, following her inside.

The sensible thing would be tell him she was too busy even for that, and to send him home. But right now, standing close beside him outside her flat, while she groped in her bag for her key, it wasn't easy to be sensible.

And once he'd taken the key from her, his hand briefly resting on hers, sending the now familiar exhilarating tingles all over her body, it was downright impossible.

She led the way up the stairs and into her home.

'It seems I'm not the only one who's been trying to get hold of you,' he remarked, looking over at the flashing light on her ansaphone as he carried her bags into the kitchen.

'It's probably only Emma, I'll get it later,' she told him.

However, they'd just put the shopping away — Jake insisted on helping — when the phone rang again.

'I'll make the coffee while you get that,' he offered.

'Thanks.'

She smiled gratefully, her body really needed a caffeine boost. The effort of trying to control her emotions was taking its toll.

She picked up the phone.

'Hello, Kendall McKenzie speaking.'

'Kendall, I've been trying to get you all evening.'

She was instantly alert as she heard the anxiety in her father's voice.

'Dad. What's happened?'

She sensed rather than saw Jake come out of the kitchen.

'The solicitor phoned me today. I'm afraid you're going to have to put your plans to move over here on hold. There are problems with Maria's finca.'

'What sort of problems?'

Jake placed a mug of coffee on the table beside her, and she smiled her thanks as she listened to her father explain that the papers weren't in order.

It seemed that Maria's husband, Salvador, had bought the land and built the house but hadn't registered it.

Furthermore, her father told her, in

Spanish law, when someone dies their property automatically passes to their children, not their spouse, unless they leave a will saying otherwise.

And Maria couldn't find Salvador's will.

'It's going to take a while to sort out, Kendall,' said her father. 'So don't make any more plans to come over yet.' He paused. 'Anyway, maybe it's for the best.'

'What do you mean?' she asked, puzzled.

'Well, are you sure you're making the right decision, moving to Spain? I know we suggested it, but that was before we knew about your boyfriend.'

'Boyfriend?'

Out of the corner of her eye she saw Jake listening.

'That man you were with when we met you in the market.'

'I told you, he's my boss.'

This was so embarrassing. Why had she let Jake talk her into inviting him in for coffee? She knew he was hanging on to every word she was saying. What must he be thinking?

'Your mother seems to think that there's something between you.' Her father coughed awkwardly. 'I must say you did seem rather . . . close.'

Kendall cringed. She could feel Jake's inquisitive eyes boring into the back of her head and hoped he couldn't hear the other side of the conversation. Her father had a tendency to speak rather loud, based on the theory that, as Spain was so far away, he needed to shout to be heard.

'Look, Dad, thanks for letting me know. I suppose I'll just have to wait to see whether Maria's paperwork turns up. Otherwise, I'll have to look for another villa. Maybe you're right. I'll just put my plans to move on hold for now.'

'I think that would be the wisest thing to do. We're just about to go out, dear, so I'll have to go, but I'll keep you up to date with any news.'

'OK. 'Bye, Dad.'

She put down the phone and turned to face Jake, knowing that he'd heard enough to make him curious.

'Trouble?' He raised an eyebrow enquiringly.

'There's a bit of a problem with the property I'm buying in Spain,' she told him, briefly relating what her father had said.

'And that bit about me?'

She felt her cheeks flush.

'Mum and Dad got the wrong impression when they saw us together,' she said, hoping she sounded casual. 'They seem to think there's something between us.'

'I see. And you disagree?' he asked softly.

She bit her lip.

'I ... well ... ' she stopped in mid-sentence, her eyes widening as he got up and walked towards her, a serious look in his eyes.

'Because if you do, I'll have to show you just how wrong you are,' he said, pulling her into his arms.

A Tempting Offer

Kendall was beautiful, Jake thought, as he sprawled on the sofa, his arms around her, her head resting on his chest. But it wasn't her beauty that attracted him. He'd dated beautiful women before. It was something else. Some quality she had that he couldn't put his finger on.

He hadn't intended to come here tonight but hadn't been able to stop himself. And when she wasn't at home he'd driven himself mad with tortured thoughts that she was with someone else or had been in an accident.

Then she'd arrived, laden with shopping, and he'd wanted to take her into his arms right there and then.

All day he'd been telling himself to keep his distance, that he was playing with fire if he kept seeing her, so he'd deliberately not returned to the office.

But she was on his mind and under his skin and he had to see her.

He sighed and lightly traced the line of her cheek with his finger. He should have kept away because whenever he was near her all he wanted to do was kiss her, hold her. And when he did that he never wanted to let her go. He wanted to be with her forever, to take care of her, to love her in sickness and in health, for better, for worse, the whole works.

He loved her so much.

Hey, where had all that come from?

He sat up with a jerk, alarmed.

Of course he didn't love her. He didn't believe in love. It destroyed people. It made you want to do anything for that special person; it made you want to give them your heart so they could walk all over it. Like his father had given his heart to his stepmother.

Kendall opened her eyes and as her gaze met his, he suddenly knew that he would do anything for her and that she already had his heart.

There was no denying it. He'd fallen in love with her.

Heck! What was he going to do?

She smiled and reached out for him, her arms winding around his neck.

Melting in her embrace, Jake knew that he was lost.

'Kendall,' he murmured, pulling himself away.

'Hmm?'

She turned to look at him, her face still flushed from their kissing.

'Don't go to Spain, even if the deal works out with Maria's villa. Stay here with me.' The words were out before he could stop them.

'Why?' she asked, her emerald eyes staring into his, searching his soul.

If he told her that he loved her would that drive her away? Send her running to catch the next flight to Spain? She'd made it plain that she was the eternal bachelor girl, but maybe if he took it slowly, showed her how much he cared, maybe she would come to love him, too.

'Because we're good together,' he

told her. 'We've got something special and I think we should give it a chance.'

The silence stretched between them for what seemed like an eternity. He could hear his heart pounding in his chest.

Jake Newman, you might be about to be rejected for the first time in your life, he told himself. Steel yourself. Take it like a man.

Then she smiled, a beautiful smile that lit up her face and gave his heart wings.

'OK,' she agreed.

She pulled his head down to kiss her again and he was caught up in the heady spiral of love.

⋆　⋆　⋆

As she drove to the office the next morning, Kendall thought about Jake's words to her the night before — that they'd got something good together and that he thought that they should give it a chance.

He hadn't actually said he loved her, but he did care for her, she was sure of that, and he'd asked her to stay and not to move to Spain.

Maybe if she took it slowly and made no demands on him, he would come to love her. Or maybe not. It was a chance she had to take.

She floated on a cloud of happiness all day. Jake had a meeting and a business lunch so she didn't see much of him, but the few kisses they'd exchanged before he left the office that morning were enough to keep her happiness bubbling.

The strength of her feelings frightened her. She didn't want to get hurt and she knew that Jake had the power to hurt her now that she'd given him her heart — even though he didn't know it and she intended to keep it that way.

Play it cool, she told herself. But when Jake returned to the office later that afternoon, wrapped his arms around her and planted a kiss on her mouth that turned her bones to jelly, she knew that she was way past playing it cool.

'I have to go to London for a business meeting tomorrow, so I'm not going to be able to take these papers into Gareth Stokes, the managing director at Morgan D'Arcy. Would you mind taking them for me? Just make sure you ask the receptionist to give them to Gareth personally, and that you get a receipt for them. OK?'

He placed a buff-coloured folder on her desk. These must be the details of the new computer programme that EXA Electronics would be installing.

'No problem.' She was secretly thrilled that he trusted her to do something as important as this. 'I'll take them first thing.'

'Ten o'clock will be early enough.' He pulled her into his arms again. 'I'm going to miss you, but I'll be back tomorrow. Why don't you come round to my place for a meal tomorrow evening? I can cook, you know,' he added, seeing her raised eyebrows.

'It's a date,' she told him.

* * *

The first thought on Kendall's mind when she woke up next morning was that she couldn't wait to see him again. She headed for work with a spring in her step.

She'd been kept busy the previous evening making the bracelet for Pete's mum, but at least it had kept her mind from dwelling on Jake.

It had taken her until past midnight to finish the bracelet, but it was worth it. It was one of the best pieces of jewellery she had ever made.

She thought of how much she'd been looking forward to moving to Spain, buying Maria's finca and having her own business. Was she being stupid to give up on her dreams so easily?

She shook her head; she'd changed her mind because she wanted to be with Jake. Like he'd said, they had something special and she didn't want to lose it. Not yet. Whenever she thought of him a warm feeling flooded through her. She loved him. She had to admit that, if only to herself. And he wanted her to stay with him. For now.

It wouldn't last, she knew that, but she was prepared to take however much of his heart he was willing to offer to her.

She sighed. In a few weeks — months if she was lucky — when Jake dropped her, would she regret having changed her plans?

You've only postponed your plans, not changed them, she told herself. She knew Jake didn't love her and, with his track record, one day, probably very soon, he would tire of her.

She vowed that as soon as she saw the first sign of him losing interest she would say goodbye and leave. She wouldn't give him the satisfaction of knowing how much she was hurting. She'd just take herself off to Spain, out of his life.

But, this was no time to daydream, she reminded herself. She had a busy day in front of her. Opening her dressing-table drawer, she took out a small black box and carefully placed the bracelet inside.

Then she showered and dressed carefully, aware that she was representing Jake's company when she went to Morgan D'Arcy to hand over the proposal. She didn't want to let him down.

Selecting a navy suit with a fitted jacket that made her look smart but sassy, she matched it with a simple cream top.

She opened her jewellery case and scanned its contents. It wouldn't be proper to wear a lot of costume jewellery with her business clothes but her pride made her want to wear one of her best pieces to the Morgan D'Arcy headquarters, even if it was only a ring.

After a bit of deliberation she selected a silver orbit ring made from welded links. It was eye-catching yet discreet. She slipped it on to her finger, selected a classy pair of silver drop earrings, and popped the case containing the bracelet into her handbag, ready to give Pete at lunch time as she'd arranged.

★   ★   ★

She arrived at Morgan D'Arcy just before ten o'clock and went to reception to hand over the proposal.

'Would you please make sure that Gareth Stokes gets these papers as soon as possible?' she asked the receptionist. 'And Mr Newman would like a receipt for them, please.'

'If those are the figures from EXA Electronics, I'll take them now.'

She turned to see a middle-aged, portly gentleman standing beside her.

He smiled at her and extended his hand. 'I'm Gareth Stokes.'

'Kendall McKenzie, Mr Newman's PA.'

She shook his hand then gave him the buff folder.

'I'm pleased to be able to hand this to you personally, Mr Stokes.'

'Thank you.' He placed the folder under his arm. 'Would you like to come into my office and wait while I scan through it?'

'Of course.'

So this was the top man himself! Well, it was good of him to take such a personal interest. Jake would be pleased when she told him.

'Could you arrange for coffee to be sent to my office, please?' Mr Stokes asked the receptionist.

'Certainly, sir.'

'This way, my dear,' he told Kendall. He led the way into his room and invited her to sit down while he skimmed through the figures to see if he had any queries.

The coffee soon arrived and she sipped it gratefully as she studied the jewellery catalogue that had been left on a side table. Morgan D'Arcy certainly did an exclusive range of jewellery. No wonder many of their clients were the rich and famous.

'This is very impressive,' Gareth Stokes finally announced. 'I'll have the figures checked, of course, but you can tell Jake we've got a deal in principle. If there are any points I need to discuss with him, then I'll contact him later.'

'Thank you,' she said, smiling.

Putting the coffee cup down on the small table beside her she picked up her bag and stood up, ready to leave.

Mr Stokes also stood up and held out his hand to her. She put out her hand to shake his and he lifted it towards him.

'What an unusual ring,' he said admiringly. 'Would you mind telling me where you bought it?'

She flushed slightly at his praise. 'I . . . er . . . made it myself.'

He looked surprised. 'This is your own design?'

'Yes, I've been making my own jewellery for a few years now.'

'Would you mind if I had a closer look?'

Flattered, she slipped the ring off her finger and handed it to him.

He went back to his desk, picked up the jeweller's magnifying glass that was lying there, and peered closely through it at the ring.

'This is very well-made,' he said, when he'd finished his scrutiny. 'Do you have any other jewellery with you that you've made yourself?'

'My earrings,' she told him, flicking back her hair to reveal the silver Celtic drops.

Then she remembered Pete's mother's fiftieth birthday gift. 'And this bracelet.' She opened her handbag, took out the box and handed it to him.

She waited as he studied the bracelet carefully for a few minutes.

This man's opinion was important to her — if she hadn't got what it took to make it in the jewellery trade then it was best to know now.

'You're very talented,' he said. 'What are you doing working as a secretary when you can design and make jewellery like this?'

'I'm saving enough money to set up my own business,' she told him boldly. 'In a year or so I hope to be able to take time off from work and concentrate on designing my own range.'

'I see.' He nodded, closing the box and handing it back to her. 'Have you thought of working for a firm like ours? We're looking for a new designer and you undoubtedly have the talent.'

Kendall stared at him incredulously. Gareth Stokes, director of Morgan D'Arcy, the top jewellery company in the UK, if not Europe, was actually offering her a job. Her mind raced, wondering what to say. It was a brilliant opportunity, but was it what she wanted? She'd always been so determined to set up her own company and go it alone. She'd always resisted any suggestions that she might work for someone else first, even for the purpose of gaining experience. But to be offered a job as a designer by Morgan D'Arcy . . .

Gareth was still talking, explaining to her what the job would entail and mentioning a very attractive and generous salary.

She listened, stunned.

'You would have a free hand to design a new jewellery collection but the designs would remain the property of Morgan D'Arcy,' he told her.

'It's very kind of you,' she started to say, but he held up his hand to silence her.

'Obviously, I'm not expecting you to make up your mind right now. Go home and think about it. You can let me know your decision tomorrow.'

He took a business card from his pocket and handed it to her.

'That's my direct number.'

'Thank you.' She took the card and put it in her handbag.

All the way back to the office, she thought about Gareth Stokes' offer. Should she take it? She didn't really fancy designing jewellery for someone else but the salary was brilliant and surely it was a step in the right direction?

She pulled into the car park of EXA Electronics, still not having made a decision. Perhaps she should talk it over with Jake first?

She knew she'd agreed to take over Joyce's job but was sure that he wouldn't want to hold her back from making a good career move.

If it *was* a good career move.

I'll run it by Jake and see what he says, she decided. It would be good to talk through such an important decision with him.

However, when she arrived back at the office, there was a message saying that he needed to stay in London a bit longer and wouldn't be back until noon the next day.

The intense disappointment she felt at hearing this proved just how strong her feelings were for him.

She deliberately didn't return his call, determined not to be clingy, and instead spent the rest of the day waiting for him to phone again, longing to hear his deep, husky voice.

She waited in vain, however.

Which just goes to show that he hasn't got it as bad for me as I have for him, she thought dismally, as she switched off her computer and prepared to drive home. He was obviously more than capable of putting her out of his mind while he concentrated on business.

Pete had also phoned her earlier to cancel lunch, saying that he and Emma would pick up the bracelet later that evening. She was pleased about that as the meeting with Gareth Stokes had taken up most of the morning and she'd really needed to work through lunch to catch up.

Besides, if she had company that evening it would stop her thinking about Jake and give her something to do other than sit waiting for him to phone.

★　★　★

Pete was delighted with the bracelet. 'I can't believe you made this yourself,' he told Kendall as he studied it admiringly. 'It's beautiful. Mum will love it.'

'She's really talented, isn't she?' Emma took the mug of coffee that Kendall passed over to her, then stared at her hand. 'Hey, did you make that gorgeous ring, too?'

'Yes. Do you like it?'

'It's lovely! Really unusual. Can I try it on?'

'Sure.'

Kendall slid the ring off her finger as Emma put the coffee cup down on the table.

'Here you are.'

'It's a bit tight for me. What do you think, Pete? Isn't it lovely?'

'It certainly is. How come you aren't working in the jewellery trade when you can make stuff like this?'

'That's what I keep asking her.'

'Actually, I was offered a job at Morgan D'Arcy today.'

She told them about her meeting

with Gareth Stokes.

'Brilliant! I hope you said yes. And if you were working for them you'd have to stay here and not move to Spain.'

'Actually, I've put off the plan to move to Spain.'

She told Emma and Pete about the problems with the paperwork relating to the finca, and that in any case, Jake had asked her to stay.

Her friends were delighted with her news.

'But I haven't made any decision yet about the offer from Morgan D'Arcy. I'm not sure if I want the job.'

'Are you totally insane? Working for a top jewellery firm with a fantastic salary. What's to think about?' Emma demanded. 'You should have got him to draft a contract there and then and signed it before he changed his mind.'

'Em's right, it's a great opportunity,' Pete agreed. 'Why are you dithering? Think how good it would be for your career.'

Kendall sighed and ran her fingers

distractedly through her hair.

'I know I'll probably never get an offer like this again, but I don't really want to work for someone else. I want my own business,' she told them. 'I don't want people making money from my designs and telling me what to do. I want to cultivate my own style, have my own label.'

'You could do that in a couple of years time,' Emma pointed out. 'But think what a great experience it would be to work at a top jewellers; how much you'd learn.'

Kendall had to admit that her friend had a point.

'What's Jake saying about it?' asked Emma. 'I bet he thinks you should jump at the chance.'

'I haven't told him yet. He's in London on business. I'm going to talk to him about it when he comes back tomorrow.'

'Well, don't make any silly decisions until you *have* talked to him. This is a wonderful opportunity for you. Don't blow it,' Emma warned her.

Maybe they were right, Kendall thought, after Pete and Emma had gone.

Maybe she should take up Gareth's offer of a job.

She hoped that Jake would phone her so that she could tell him about it.

However, she didn't hear from him all evening, not even a text message.

He was obviously tied up with business. But that didn't stop her going to bed feeling really disappointed.

* * *

Her sleep was punctuated by vivid dreams of Jake and she woke up having made two firm decisions.

One was that she was going to stop fighting her love for him and give their relationship a chance. After all, Lindsay had found love again, and Pete and Emma seemed happy together, so some relationships did work out.

The second was that she definitely

wasn't going to accept Gareth Stokes' offer of a job.

It wasn't what she wanted, and five years down the line she could still be working for Morgan D'Arcy, too scared to give up the security of regular employment and a good salary — but resenting the fact that she still didn't have her own business. She felt a lot better after making that decision.

She arrived at work that morning to find the usual pile of e-mails, faxes and telephone calls to answer, not to mention the post to deal with, so was kept too busy to watch the clock, but all the time she was waiting, alert for Jake's return, wanting to hear his footsteps along the corridor, smell his aftershave, look into those dreamy brown eyes, feel his lips on hers.

Heartbreak For Kendall

He's here! The message flashed into her mind at the very same instant the door opened. She was so attuned to him that she knew, without even turning around, that he was behind her. She waited expectantly for him to wrap his arms around her, kiss her, tell her how much he'd missed her.

'So that's why you decided to take up my offer of Joyce's job, is it? So you could worm your way in at Morgan D'Arcy's?'

The words were like darts of ice hurled at her through the air.

Puzzled, she turned around.

Jake, his arms folded across his chest, angry dark eyes staring out of a face chiselled from granite, was glaring at her.

'What?' she stammered, trying to gather her thoughts together.

'Don't act the innocent, Kendall. I've just been talking to Gareth Stokes and he told me how you showed him some of your jewellery when you went to give him the proposal yesterday and that he's offered you a job.' His mouth twisted into a sneer. 'Nicely done. Talk about seizing the moment.'

She started at him, confused. Why was he so angry? Did he think she was going to leave him in the lurch?

'I haven't accepted the job . . . '

'No, because you're holding out for more money, waiting for Gareth to offer you a higher salary, I suppose,' he retorted.

'Pardon?'

What was going on?

'You used me, Kendall.'

The harsh accusation stung.

'I did not!'

He was towering over her and she felt intimidated.

Pushing back her chair, her hands shaking, she stood up to face him, forcing herself to keep her voice calm.

'How did I use you?' she asked quietly. 'Just what have I done to make you so angry?'

'Oh, yes! Go on, act the innocent.'

He paced around the room, his hands thrust in his pockets.

'Well, that doe-eyed look won't work with me. You've been scheming behind my back all along. First, you made plans to move to Spain without even telling me — '

'I didn't need your permission!' she retorted, anger welling up inside her. 'You don't own me!'

'No, but we are seeing each other.' He turned to face her, his eyes dark. 'Doesn't that mean anything to you?'

She lifted her head and challenged him.

'Does it mean anything to you?'

He paused, swallowed, and she could see that he was fighting to control himself.

'I offered you a full-time job but you refused.'

His voice was quieter now, deadly quiet.

'Then suddenly you changed your mind. And now I know why, don't I?'

She blinked. She didn't understand what he was getting at.

'You know why. There are problems with the deeds of the property I want to buy in Spain.'

'You could have bought another property. Or stayed with your parents until the deeds were sorted out.'

'You asked me not to go!' she reminded him.

'I did, didn't I? Because I thought . . . I thought we were good together. I thought you wanted to stay here with me.'

He sounded so cold, so distant.

'That's why I offered you a permanent job.'

She shook her head, bewildered.

'Of course I wanted to stay. I wouldn't have accepted the job otherwise. Look, Jake, what's the matter?'

She reached out to him but he pulled away.

'When I first offered you Joyce's job

you refused; you were all set on going to Spain until I landed that contract with Morgan D'Arcy.'

He practically spat the words out.

'That's when you realised I could be useful to you. Here was your chance to get your foot in the door of one of the top jewellery firms.'

'I did no such thing,' she denied hotly. How dare he?

'Really?' He turned to face her, his expression stony. 'Then why did you take your jewellery with you to show Gareth Stokes? All I asked you to do was hand in the proposal form, not to have a meeting with the man and discuss your future career prospects. But you couldn't resist using the opportunity for your own ends, could you? And to think I was the one who put the idea into your head.'

'What?'

She had no idea what he was on about.

He shot her a scathing look.

'Don't pretend you've forgotten that

when we were in Spain I suggested you should show your jewellery to a leading jewellers to see if they would take you on and give you your own label.'

Oh no, she had forgotten! But he'd never believe her, she realised in dismay. He thought she'd engineered it all. That she'd taken the job with him hoping for an opportunity to show her work to Morgan D'Arcy.

She opened her mouth to deny it, then anger took over. A cold, white fury coursed through her body. How could he think that of her? She loved him, but obviously he didn't feeling the same way about her or he would never judge her so harshly.

'So that's what you think, is it?' she asked coldly.

Her eyes met his, cold emerald ice clashing with angry dark brown.

'Well, now that you know what a treacherous, devious person I really am, I'm sure you won't want anything more to do with me — so I'll save you the trouble of ending both our business and personal relationships and tell you that I quit on both accounts.'

Picking up her bag she swept out of the office.

* * *

Nice one, Jake, he thought, grimly. Now she'll go straight to Gareth Stokes and accept his offer of a job with a clear conscience, saying that she couldn't be expected to continue working for Jake after their argument. Well, it saved him the unpleasant task of sacking her. There was no way he could work with her or continue with their relationship after being betrayed like this.

He sat down at her desk, his head in his hands. She'd got what she wanted. And he'd learned a valuable lesson. Never mix business with pleasure. He'd obeyed that rule all his life and the one time he relaxed it, look what happened. That's what you get for letting down your guard and getting involved, he told himself.

If only he didn't love her.

He got up and paced the floor. He'd thought Kendall was special, that he could trust her. You were bewitched by a pretty face, he told himself.

But she'd been so angry. And so hurt.

That's what women do when you catch them out. He remembered Leticia and her wide-eyed innocence while all the while she was scheming to ruin his business and had been having an affair with his manager.

Yet Leticia's betrayal hadn't hurt like this.

He'd thought he could trust Kendall. Had been so sure of it.

★　★　★

The ice-cold anger had lasted until she got home, but as soon as she reached the sanctuary of her flat, Kendall burst into tears. How could he judge her like that without even giving her a chance to explain? Did he really think so little of her to believe that she would stoop so

264

low? Use him to get a job? Betray his trust? He had been so quick to assume that she would accept Gareth Stokes' offer, not even considering that it wasn't what she wanted.

What was that he'd said in Spain — that he didn't think she would ever knowingly let anyone down. Well, he'd soon changed his tune!

★　★　★

She phoned Gareth Stokes the next morning to decline his offer of a job, politely explaining that she wanted her own jewellery business and to market her own designs.

Gareth had told her that she had the talent to succeed and wished her luck.

His belief in her would have pleased her if only her heart hadn't been so heavy.

She had hoped that when Jake had cooled down and had thought things over, he would come after her, apologise, and give her a chance to explain.

But days passed and she heard nothing from him. It was as if he'd wiped her out of his life. The time they'd spent together had never existed.

She stared into the mirror at her pale face and red-rimmed eyes. She couldn't believe that she, Kendall McKenzie, had spent so many hours crying over a man. Her friends wouldn't believe it either. She smiled ruefully at her reflection. Jake Newman had really got under her skin. More than that, he'd made her do something she had vowed she would never do.

He'd made her fall in love with him and now he'd broken her heart.

Well, she wasn't going to stay here moping. She was going back to her original plan. She was going to pack her bags and go to Spain.

Her parents would put her up until the deeds to Maria's finca were sorted out. Or until she had found another place of her own. Then she was going to work hard at making her jewellery. Gareth Stokes thought she could do it and she was determined she would succeed. She'd show Jake. She didn't need to work for a company like Morgan D'Arcy to make her name, she would do it on her own. Just like she'd always planned.

She made a quick phone call to her parents to check that it was OK for her to stay with them for a few weeks. Her mother answered and was delighted but worried — as Kendall had known she would be — wanting to know what had happened to her job with that 'nice young man'.

Kendall fobbed her off with the explanation that the temporary position had ended sooner than expected, relieved that she'd never confided in her parents about her true feelings for Jake.

Then she booked a seat on the next available flight — on Friday morning — and after she'd phoned the estate agents to arrange for them to rent out her flat again, she set off to see Lindsay. She'd tell Emma about her change of plan later, when her friend finished work.

'Off again?' Lindsay asked, her disappointment obvious. 'But what about Jake? Emma said that the pair of you were an item now.'

'We were. Past tense,' Kendall said flatly, hoping the pain she felt wasn't showing on her face.

Lindsay shot her a concerned look.

'Oh, Kendy, poor you. You fell for him big time, didn't you?'

'Yep, for once I forgot my own rules and trusted a guy with my heart.'

She turned pain-filled eyes to her friend.

'And, true to form, he trampled on it.'

'What happened?' Lindsay asked softly.

Kendall briefly told her.

'It's just a misunderstanding. If you explained to him, he'd see how wrong he was and apologise,' Lindsay told her.

'He judged me wrongly without even asking for an explanation,' Kendall said bitterly. 'And he hasn't bothered to contact me since, which shows how little he thinks of me.'

'Or how hurt he is.'

Kendall ignored that remark.

'I love him but he doesn't love me. Jake doesn't commit to anyone. He has a 'relationship' for as long as it suits him, then it's on to the next girlfriend.'

'Maybe he's changed. After all, you've never been keen to commit to anyone, either,' Lindsay pointed out. 'Why don't you call him and explain? Give him a chance?'

'No way. I've never chased after a guy in my life and I'm not starting now.'

'So you're doing what you always do — running away.'

'I'm doing what I always wanted to do, starting my own jewellery business,' Kendall told her. 'Now can we please change the subject? I'm leaving for Spain tomorrow and I don't even want to think about Jake Newman, never mind talk about him.'

Luckily, baby Sophie chose that moment to wake from her afternoon nap and Lindsay was too busy changing her and preparing her bottle to pursue the matter.

★　★　★

Jake put down the phone, a deep frown etched across his forehead. Gareth Stokes had just phoned him from Morgan D'Arcy to discuss a few points in the proposal. In the ensuing conversation he had told Jake how disappointed he was that Kendall had refused his offer of a job, but she hadn't been very enthusiastic in the first place, so he'd half expected her to decline.

Gareth had gone on to say how lucky Jake was to have a secretary like her but how he thought her talent was wasted working in an office. She should be designing jewellery.

It was then Jake found out that Kendall had been about to leave the proposal with the secretary in reception when Gareth had seen her and insisted that she waited while he went through it.

He recalled Gareth's words, 'I noticed the lovely ring she was wearing and asked her where she'd bought it. She told me she'd made it herself so I asked if she had any more items of jewellery with her and she showed me her earrings and a bracelet she'd made for a friend's mother. I was amazed. They're incredible pieces.'

So he'd been wrong. Jake sighed. She hadn't wrangled a meeting with Gareth so she could show him her jewellery. He hadn't been used or betrayed. She'd just been wearing a ring and some earrings of her own — as she always did. And she'd had the bracelet in her handbag because she'd arranged to give it to Pete that lunch time.

While Jake was trying to decide what to do about the mess he'd created, the phone had rung again. This time it was Tanya, his friend Hugh's fiancée, calling to tell him that she'd heard that Kendall was flying to Spain the next day. She was renting out her flat and going over there to live.

'You're going to lose her, Jake, if you don't do something about it,' Tanya had told him. 'And don't tell me you don't care about her because I know you do.'

He hadn't bothered to deny it, but had replied that if Kendall wanted to go to live in Spain that it was up to her. It was her choice.

And his loss.

Well, he'd get over it. Just like she obviously had. She was going to Spain to follow her dream and was leaving him behind without so much as a goodbye.

He wanted to call her and say he was sorry; beg her not to go. But he wouldn't. If Kendall McKenzie thought so little of him that she was prepared to leave him and live in Spain then let her get on with it.

★　★　★

Kendall glanced at her watch as she waited in the departures lounge with twenty minutes to go before her flight was due to be called. She'd spent a sleepless night thinking about Jake. How she longed to see him again, to hear his voice say her name, to feel his mouth on hers, his arms around her.

Get over it, he doesn't love you, she told herself. Men like Jake never love anyone. They're too scared of getting hurt. Just like she had been, she thought ruefully.

She opened up the newspaper she'd bought and tried to read it, but all she could see was Jake's face. Her heart ached as she remembered that weekend in Spain. They had been so close. And now it was as if they had never known each other, never kissed, never embraced so passionately.

She had to stop thinking about him. It was driving her crazy. She was starting a new life, a new business. She had everything to look forward to. She would push him to the back of her mind and keep him there until thinking about him wasn't so raw.

She forced herself to look at the

newspaper, even though she couldn't take in the words. Her eyes were on the open page but her mind was elsewhere.

Then the loudspeaker announcing her flight number broke through her troubled thoughts and she picked up her bags.

There was no time for doubts now. She had a plane to catch.

Slowly, she walked down the corridor and — passport and boarding pass at the ready — joined the long queue at the departure gate.

Emma had wanted to come and see her off but Kendall hated goodbyes.

She preferred to go quietly, alone. Nursing her broken heart.

It was almost her turn now. Just two people in front of her. She wanted to turn around and go back, talk to Jake, make him understand that he'd judged her wrongly but her pride wouldn't let her. If he'd cared he'd have asked her what had happened, not jumped to conclusions.

She bit her lip; she had to admit that

on the surface it had looked bad. OK, it was sheer coincidence that she'd agreed to take the job as his secretary just as he'd been offered the contract with Morgan D'Arcy, and another coincidence that she'd bumped into Gareth Stokes in reception and he'd insisted on looking through the proposal himself.

She shook her head. No. She wouldn't make excuses for Jake. He should have trusted her, or at least listened to her, and allowed her to explain. He obviously didn't love her. It hurt but she would get over it. It wouldn't hurt forever.

Would it?

Goodbye, Jake.

Her parents had been delighted to see her but, amazingly — because it was obvious how upset Kendall was despite her efforts to put on a brave face — her mother had resisted the urge to question her or even fuss over her.

Both her parents had made her welcome but had given her space, allowing the beauty of the surroundings and the warmth of the Spanish sunshine to ease the pain in her heart.

She gazed out of her bedroom window at the orange and lemon trees dotted about the coarse wild grass, and wished she'd never met Jake Newman.

She'd been there a week now and there had been no word from him, although both Tanya and Lindsay had phoned to see how she was settling in, and had tried to persuade her to go back. Tanya had managed to slip into the conversation the fact that Jake had sounded devastated when he'd heard she'd gone to Spain.

'I was sure he'd come after you,' she'd said.

'Why should he? We'd only known each other for a couple of weeks,' Kendall had reminded her.

She could hardly believe that was all it had been. She felt like she'd known him forever, would miss him forever.

And if this was what love felt like then she never wanted to love anyone again.

But she needed to pull herself together and get on with her life, and she resolved to make a start that day by looking at the situations vacant column in the local paper. If there were no vacancies for English language teachers, then she'd advertise private English lessons.

She had to start earning some money, and keeping herself busy would take her mind off Jake.

She'd forget him in time.

A knock on the door interrupted her thoughts.

'Kendall?'

It was her father.

She turned away from the window and forced a smile on to her face.

'Come in, Dad.'

He opened the door and stepped inside.

'The solicitor has just phoned. Maria has found Salvador's will, clearly stating that the deeds of the property pass to her on his death, and the house registration is being sorted out. The solicitor is giving it urgent priority so you should be able to go ahead with the purchase of the finca in a couple of weeks — if you still want to?'

This was just the good news she needed! Now she could throw herself into setting up her business and push Jake Newman right out of her mind.

'Yes, I do still want to go ahead. That's great, Dad. And how long will it take to set up the mortgage?'

'Brian's friend says that it's all in

place. You'll get a formal offer within the next couple of days.'

'Good.'

'Are you sure this is what you want, Kendall?' Her father's face was etched with concern. 'Your mother and I can't help feeling that something's troubling you. Don't make a hasty decision, love, just because you're upset over something . . . or someone.'

She smiled ruefully.

'Nothing escapes your eagle eye, does it? Yes, I have had a bit of a fall out with Jake, the man I worked for. We dated a few times but it was nothing serious. And it's made me realise that this is what I want to do. I'll always regret it if I let this opportunity pass by.'

And what about Jake? she asked herself. Will you regret letting him pass by?

But he knew where she was, and if he thought so little of her then she was better off without him.

'If you're sure?' her father asked gently.

'Positive.' She nodded emphatically. 'The sooner I can buy Maria's house the better.'

'Well, in that case, I've heard that the Language Institute in Marbella are looking for English teachers. A job there would tide you over for a while. Perhaps you'd like to phone them and ask for an application form?'

'I'll do better than that,' she told him. 'I'll drive over there and hand in my CV. Then I'll take a look around the shops. I might be able to pick up some bits and pieces of materials that I need for my jewellery. I'm almost out of clasps and I could do with getting myself another wire jig.'

The thought of a trip to Marbella cheered her up immensely. She needed to get out; to do something positive and stop dwelling on how things might have been. It would never have worked out with Jake. She had to move on.

★　★　★

Jake thrust his hands into his pockets and gazed thoughtfully out of the office window. Kendall had been gone over a week now but the pain was still raw. He couldn't believe he missed her so much. How had she wrapped herself around his heart in such a short time?

The buzzing of the intercom on his desk interrupted his thoughts. It was the temporary secretary from the agency. She was very efficient, and attractive too, but nothing like Kendall. There again, he'd never met anyone else like Kendall. She was so alive, so vibrant . . . The buzzer sounded more urgently.

He sighed, walked over to the desk and pressed the button.

'Yes, Miss Swanson?'

'Your father is on the line, Mr Newman. Shall I put him through?'

'Yes, please.'

So his father had returned from his holiday in Switzerland? Jake wondered if he had got wind of that problem in

Marbella, or had heard about the crisis in the US office that he'd just managed to diffuse. Well, at least everything was back under control. The last thing his father needed with his weak heart was a load of business worries.

He picked up the receiver as soon as the phone rang.

'Dad. How are you? How was your holiday?'

'I'm good. Fit as a fiddle,' his father's voice boomed in his ear. 'Can you meet me for lunch at Figaro's? It's about time I caught up with what's happening in the company.'

'Yes, of course, I can make it for one o'clock. And don't worry about the business, Dad, everything is fine.'

'Glad to hear it. See you at one o'clock, then. I'll book our usual table.'

A gentle click announced that his father had ended the call.

He sounded much better, Jake thought with relief. He'd been so worried about him — his health had never been the same since Melanie had got her hooks into him.

Which just goes to show you the dangers of falling in love, Jake reminded himself. Love made you weak, made you see only the good in people, made you trust blindly. Like he'd trusted Kendall.

But she'd done nothing to break that trust, had she?

He'd simply misjudged her.

Maybe he should have gone after her and apologised. Surely he owed her that much?

He shook his head, trying to clear his thoughts. He owed her nothing. She'd chosen to leave. She'd always intended to go Spain and wouldn't even have told him about it if he hadn't offered her a permanent job. She'd made it clear she didn't want to be tied down. She was probably too busy with her new life and new business to even think about him. He shrugged his shoulders and returned to the pile of paperwork on his desk — it would be another two hours before he met his father for lunch so he might as well put the time to good use.

* * *

His father was already at the restaurant when Jake arrived.

'Jake! You look tired. Not been overworking, I hope?' his father asked, rising from his seat to greet him.

'We've had a couple of problems, but they're sorted out now. There's nothing for you to worry about.'

'Yes, I heard about the business with Clavero Sistemas in Spain. I never did like that Leticia, but I didn't think she'd be so treacherous. Still, you know what they say about a woman scorned.'

He resumed his seat and Jake sat down opposite him.

'We never had a serious relationship, Dad, and she knew it. I laid my cards on the table right at the beginning. I never promised her anything.'

His father picked up a bottle of wine from the table and poured some into the empty glass in front of Jake.

'Maybe not, but she obviously wanted more. You have to be careful with women like Leticia — and Melanie. They're beautiful, charming and only out for what they can get.'

'Don't worry, I don't intend to let any woman get close enough to me to hurt me like that,' Jake reassured him. 'Love's for fools.'

His father frowned. 'I'm sorry you think that way, son. To be in love with someone who loves you back is a wonderful thing. Look at your mother; I'd have trusted her with my life and we had many happy years together. My mistake was to try to regain that love with a shallow, money-grabber like Melanie.' He paused to take a sip of his wine. 'I should have known better but I missed your mother so much I'm afraid I wasn't thinking straight. I was just grateful to find someone else to care for me, to fill in the lonely hours.'

In his anger at how Melanie had taken his father for a ride, Jake had forgotten how happy his parents had been. Melanie and Leticia were of the same mould, he acknowledged, just out for what they could get — they both looked on a man as a trophy. Whereas his mother had been kind and supportive; the sort of person you could rely on. Like Kendall.

The thought stunned him for a moment. He remembered how Kendall had been upfront with him right from the start. How she'd told him of her dreams of starting a jewellery design business; how she'd been the soul of discretion in Marbella; how she had turned down the offer to work for Morgan D'Arcy; how hurt she'd looked when he'd accused her of deceiving him. And how he'd let her walk out of his life.

'I hope I haven't put you off getting married, son,' his father was saying. 'There's nothing I'd like better than to see you settle down. If you're ever lucky enough to find a good woman who loves you back, you must make sure you don't let her go. If you turn your back on love you're a fool because life is pretty empty without it.'

Did Kendall love him? If she did, then surely she wouldn't have gone off like that? She could have tried to explain. Surely she could see how it looked to him? She hadn't tried to get in touch, and it had been well over a week since she'd walked out of his office.

As the thoughts tumbled around in his head, he realised that his father was still speaking to him.

'So the doctor has given me the all clear to return to work and I'm coming back into the office starting on Monday.'

'You are?' Jake was instantly alert. 'Are you sure you're up to it? Are you coming back full-time?'

'I certainly am 'up to it' as you say. I'm not in my dotage yet.' His father's eyes twinkled. 'And I'm fully aware of the sacrifices you made to take care of my company. I really appreciate it, Jake, you did a marvellous job and kept EXA from going under. But I'm fit and I need something to keep me occupied, so I'm ready to pick up the reins again.'

He leaned over and patted Jake's shoulder.

'If you want to go back to running that website business of yours, that's fine by me. Of course, there's always a place for you at EXA and I'd be glad if you could see your way to coming into the office a couple of days a week.'

'That's excellent, Dad.' Jake felt his heart lifting.

His father was back and he was free to get on with his own life again.

★   ★   ★

It had been a mistake to go into Marbella, Kendall acknowledged when she returned home. It had reminded her too much of Jake and the time they'd spent there together. The Language Institute was just around the corner from the hotel where they'd stayed and to her chagrin she couldn't help herself driving past it, remembering the days they'd spent there and how close they'd been that last weekend.

Not close enough for him to trust you or even to listen to your side of things, she reminded herself, as she took her shopping up to her room. But then she hadn't told him her side of things, had she? She'd just walked out.

Her parents weren't at home, they were lunching with friends. They certainly had a busy social life! Quite a few ex-pats had moved from other parts of Spain to Antiquera where the property was cheaper and the way of life slower.

She left her purchases on her bed and went to make herself a cup of coffee and a sandwich.

When she'd finished her lunch she gathered together all her jewellery materials. Her father had offered her the use of his shed until the purchase of the finca came though and she was going to take him up on it. She already had some ideas for new designs and she wanted to make some sketches while they were still fresh in her mind. She intended to keep herself busy; too busy to think of Jake. She wasn't going to waste any more time on someone who cared so little about her.

★   ★   ★

Kendall worked hard all afternoon, rarely coming out of the shed.

So, next day, her mother took some lunch to her on a tray — just to make sure she ate something. Kendall's parents were going out for the day, and her mum knew she wouldn't bother to go to the house to prepare anything for herself.

'Don't overdo it, dear, you're looking a bit peaky,' her mother told her as she took her a pasta salad and a jug of fresh orange juice. 'Why don't you come into Puerto Banus with us? The market's on today. You'd enjoy a rummage about the stalls.'

'No, thanks.' Kendall barely looking up from the sketch of a brooch that she was working on, and so her mother left her to get on with it.

She wanted to work. Had to work. Then, when she got into bed at night, she might be too exhausted to think. But, although she sometimes managed to keep Jake from her thoughts in the day, at night he was always there, filling her head, taking over her dreams.

The sketch now finished, she decided to start making the brooch right away. Some of the gemstones she'd bought in Marbella would be ideal for it.

She took the stones out of their box and had just laid them out on the workbench when there was a knock on the shed door.

She sighed, surely her parents weren't going to make another attempt to persuade her to go out with them?

'Come in,' she called, her attention still focused on the bench in front of her.

She heard the door open, and then a

sudden, familiar tingling at the back of her neck made her look round.

'Jake!'

She stared at him in amazement, her heart flipping as it always did when she saw him. He looked just as incredibly handsome as she remembered, if a little tired around the eyes. He'd probably been overworking, as usual. What was he doing here?

'Hello, Kendall. I arrived just as your parents were leaving. They said it would be OK for me to see you.'

I bet they did, she thought. They'd probably guessed she'd been moping over Jake and were now hoping things would be sorted out.

She didn't trust herself to stand up, her legs felt too wobbly to support her, so she remained seated and gave him what she hoped was a cool, enquiring look.

'What can I do for you?'

'Can we go somewhere else to talk?' he asked. 'It's a bit cramped in here.'

He did seem to dwarf the place. The

shed was quite large but there hardly seemed room to breathe with him in there. And her heart was beating so loudly that she was sure he could hear it.

He still had the same effect on her.

She took a deep breath and forced herself to speak calmly.

'I'm not sure that we actually have anything to talk about. But we can go into the house if you want.'

Now why had she said that when she knew her legs were wobbling like jelly?

'Thanks, I appreciate it.'

He held the shed door open and waited for her.

She hoped he had no idea of the effort it took for her to stand up, make her way over to the door and then walk out ahead of him.

'Your mother said she'd leave us a snack and had put the coffee machine on,' he told her as he fell into step beside her.

He must have had quite a conversation with her mother.

She could just imagine the looks that had passed between her parents when he'd turned up, and what would be the main topic of their conversation as they drove to see their friends.

The smell of fresh coffee greeted her as soon as she walked into the kitchen. Two of her mum's best china cups and saucers had been left next to a plate of sandwiches covered in cling film. No matter what the occasion, her mother was always prepared.

'Take a seat. So, what's brought you here?' she asked in what she hoped was a casual, unconcerned tone as she poured the coffee. 'Business?'

'No. I came to see you.'

That took her by surprise.

She quickly steadied her hand and put down her cup before all the coffee went into the saucer.

'Why?'

'To apologise.' He put down his cup too, and looked her straight in the face. 'The things I said to you, accused you of . . . I was wrong . . . I'm sorry.'

'Yes, you were wrong,' she acknowledged, returning his gaze steadily. 'But it's taken you long enough to realise that. I suppose you finally decided to ask Gareth Stokes about it?'

Jake looked a little shamefaced. 'Actually, Gareth phoned me the next day to discuss the contract you'd delivered. He said how disappointed he was that you'd turned down the job but he'd been half expecting it as he could see that you weren't interested. He told me what happened, how you'd been about to leave when he called you back, how he'd noticed your jewellery . . . ' Jake paused, his brown eyes solemn. 'I'm so sorry, Kendall. I should have trusted you.'

'Why? You barely know me,' she pointed out. 'I don't blame you for not trusting me after what Leticia did. But you could have asked me about it; given me a chance to explain.'

Then she realised what he'd said. Gareth Stokes had told him the very next day what had happened. Yet he'd done nothing; had left her to flee to Spain, broken-hearted.

Only he didn't know she was broken-hearted, did he? And he was never going to, either.

'Hang on, you knew the truth before I left for Spain?' she said, anger welling up inside her. 'Yet you've left it for nearly two whole weeks to apologise? So why have you decided to come now?'

She was angry, he could tell by the dangerous flash in her emerald eyes, by the tightness of her lips. Well he didn't blame her. He should have apologised as soon as he'd found out he'd misjudged her.

'You're right, I should have come sooner. I wish I had. But I'm here now. Will you forgive me? I've missed you, Kendy, I was hoping we could carry on seeing each other?'

She could hardly believe her ears. He wanted her to start dating him again yet he thought so little of her that it had taken him all this time to get around to apologising for accusing her of deceiving him and of lying and cheating.

She stood up. 'I'm sorry, but I couldn't possibly go out with anyone who has so little respect for me that he jumps to conclusions without hearing my side of the story, and then when he finds out he was wrong doesn't even have the courtesy to apologise straight away.'

She walked over to the back door and opened it. She turned to him.

'Goodbye, Jake.'

Together Forever

Thank goodness he hadn't made a complete fool of himself and told her that he loved her, Jake thought, looking at Kendall's stony face. He must have been mad to come all the way over here. Why hadn't he just written her a letter to apologise? Or phoned her? Whatever had possessed him to leave the restaurant after that meal with his father and book himself on the next available flight to Spain?

Because you wanted to see her again, he reminded himself. Well, now you have and it's obvious she doesn't feel the same way about you, so get out of here while you still have some dignity left, he told himself.

'Very well.' He rose from his chair and walked over to the door.

As he passed her, Kendall quickly averted her face but not before he saw her chin quiver and the glint of a tear in her eye.

She was upset, he realised, and it was his fault.

He paused, unsure of what to do.

'Look, I'm sorry. You're right. I should have apologised to you sooner. I didn't mean to hurt you,' he added softly

'Don't worry about it. I'm sure you have more important things to concern yourself with than apologising to your former *temporary* secretary.'

Her voice was laced with sarcasm and she was still avoiding his eyes.

Could it be that she did care about him after all?

He took a deep breath. He was about to do something he had never done before in all his life but he knew that if he didn't do it now then he would always regret it.

'You're more than that to me,' he said, gently cupping her chin with his right hand and turning her face towards him. 'I love you, Kendall.'

There, he'd said it.

He saw the mixture of surprise, delight, and then suspicion in her eyes as she stared at him.

'What d-did you say?' she stammered.

He cupped both his hands around her face now, drew her towards him and kissed her, gently at first. Then, as she responded, he kissed her ever more passionately until they both broke away, breathless.

'I said, I love you,' he repeated. 'That's why I didn't come to apologise before. I was too scared.'

'Scared?' Kendall felt like she was living in a dream. First he told her he loved her, then he told her that he had been too scared to come to see her. None of it made sense. She shook her head in bewilderment, running her hands through her tousled hair.

'Scared of what? Of me?'

Jake nodded. 'I didn't want to love you. Didn't want to love anyone. I like to be in control of my emotions. If you love someone you give them the power to hurt you. Especially if they don't love you back. And I was scared that you might not love me.'

He looked at her.

'Do you?' he asked softly. 'Do you love me, Kendall?'

She was still trying to get her head around it. Jake loved her. Jake Newman — Mr No Commitments — millionaire and eternal playboy had flown all the way to Spain to apologise for misjudging her and to tell her he loved her. And he wanted to know if she loved him. She guessed she owed him the truth about that one.

She nodded slowly. 'Yes, I do. I do love you. And I'm scared, too,' she admitted. 'I've seen so many people fall in love and get hurt. I promised I wouldn't ever let it happen to me.'

'I won't ever hurt you,' he promised.

He pulled her to him once more and kissed her lips softly again, wrapping his arms around her, enveloping her in his love.

She returned his kiss, then nestled her head against his shoulder, revelling in his nearness. She didn't want this moment to end or to have to think about what to do next.

'You know, I think I fell in love with you the very first time I saw you, when you bashed into me with that buggy,' he told her, kissing her on the top of her head.

She smiled as she remembered that moment. And her first reaction to him.

He'd gotten to her right from the start, too.

'I think I felt the same way,' she confessed. 'Yet I always thought love at first sight was a load of twaddle.'

He laughed. 'And I, my darling, thought love itself was a load of twaddle until you came into my life and turned it upside down.'

Well, they'd admitted their love for each other, so what happens now?

Did Jake want her to go back to England with him? And if he did, would she?

Of course she would. She couldn't bear to be apart from him — the last couple of weeks had shown her that.

For once in her life she had to take a chance on loving someone. She didn't know if it would work out. They were poles apart — Jake was a business tycoon and she was just a struggling English teacher and small-time jewellery designer, but she did know she had to give their love a chance.

'Well, now that we both know how we feel, there's only one thing for it. We'll have to get married.'

'What?' She lifted her head to stare at him, saw the love shining out of his eyes and knew that he was deadly serious. 'Are you proposing to me?'

'I am.' He released her, and got down on one knee. 'Kendall McKenzie, would you do me the honour of being my wife?'

He was actually asking her to marry him. What should she say?

Follow your heart just for once in your life, Kendy.

'Yes,' she whispered, her heart soaring. 'Yes, I will!'

She heard him whoop with triumph, then she was in his arms yet again and being smothered by his kisses.

'Let's go choose a ring right away,' he told her when they finally came up for air. 'Then we can set a date and book the church . . . you do want a church wedding, don't you?'

She placed her finger over his lips and smiled. 'Let's not rush this, Jake. There are things we need to discuss first.'

'Like what?' His eyes clouded over. 'You're not having second thoughts, are you?'

She shook her head. 'No . . . but what about the finca I'm buying . . . my jewellery business . . . I can't give it all up.'

'Surely you don't still want to live in Spain?'

Did she? She thought about it and realised that she didn't. She wanted to marry Jake, to live with him. But she did want to carry on with her plans for her new career.

'No, I don't think I ever really wanted to live in Spain. I was just running away from you,' she admitted. 'But I do want to design my own jewellery. Marrying you doesn't mean I intend to give up my dreams.'

'Won't you be too busy running our home, organising business lunches for my clients and getting involved with deserving charities, to have time for all that?' he asked. 'After all, there's no need for you to work. I've got more than enough money to keep us.'

She stared at him, aghast. Is that what he expected her to do? She thought of all the other businessmen's wives she'd seen, immaculately coiffured, elegantly dressed, bored out of their minds. She couldn't live like that. Not even for Jake.

'That's not what I want to do, Jake,' her voice was low and apologetic as she pulled away from him. 'I'm afraid that if you're after a wife like that then I'm not the one for you.'

She swallowed down the lump forming in her throat. She should have known it was too good to be true. He was out of her league. He might love her but they came from two different worlds.

'But I don't want a wife like that,' he said, his voice laced with laughter. 'I want one just like you. Fiery and independent.' He reached out to pull her back towards him and kissed her on the forehead. 'Beautiful and very, very talented.'

'Why you!' she clenched her fist and thumped him playfully on the chest.

'And I'm pleased that you still want to design jewellery because I want you to be a partner in my new company.'

'What company?'

'My jewellery company. I was hoping you could help me think of a name for it. Oh, and I need a good designer. It's a great job. She gets a life-time contract, her own label, a free hand to make all her own designs and half the profits. Interested?'

Was she interested? You bet she was.

'And what are you going to do?' she teased. 'Be my secretary?'

'No, darling, I'm going to follow my dream too. You see, my father has finally got over his broken heart and is coming back to EXA. I'll still keep an eye on things, of course, but I'll only be working for him a couple of days a week. I'm going back to website design and the first thing I'm going to do is design a website for your jewellery company.'

'So we're both getting our dream?' she asked.

'That's right,' he said, kissing her on the nose.

But it was all with Jake's money, Kendall suddenly realised. He was the one who was making her dream come true. She wriggled away a little and looked at him seriously.

'I'll sell my flat and put my money into the business too,' she told him. 'And, Jake, I think I ought to sign a prenuptial agreement before we get married. You know, so that if it doesn't work out you get to keep your money.'

'There is no way I am asking my wife to sign a prenuptial agreement.' Jake sounded furious. 'When we get married we share everything. Do you understand?'

'But, Jake, you've got more to share than I have,' she pointed out. All she had was her flat.

'Look, I'm sorry that I'm a rich man, as it obviously bothers you so much, but we either enter this marriage with the belief that it's forever or we don't do it at all. Agreed?'

His eyes held hers and she felt the love flowing between them, so intense that she could almost reach out and touch it. He was right, she realised. It had to be total commitment. No more running away. For either of them.

'Agreed,' she said softly.

She saw his face relax and he moved closer again, winding his arm around her waist. 'Anyway, you're forgetting that I'm gaining something really special out of this marriage,' he murmured.

'What's that?' she asked.

'You,' he said.

Then his mouth claimed hers and they were both too busy to do any more talking.

'Do I take it that the news that Maria's son wants to buy her finca as a holiday home won't come as too big a disappointment to you, Kendall?' her father's amused voice butted in.

Heck! She hadn't heard her mum and dad come back! How long had they been standing there?

She tried to wriggle out of Jake's arms but he held on to her fiercely, turning so that his arm was around her shoulders as they both faced her grinning parents.

'Mr and Mrs McKenzie,' he said proudly. 'I've just asked your daughter to marry me and she's accepted. I hope you both approve?'

'I told you, didn't I, John?' her

mother said in delight. 'I knew he was the one for Kendall as soon as I saw the two of them together.'

'You did, Anna. And, as usual, you were right.' Her father held out his hand to Jake. 'Welcome to the family, son.'

THE END

ELUSIVE LOVE

Karen Abbott

Amelia has always been determined to marry for love . . . but with her elder brother dead and posthumously branded as a traitor, Amelia and her sister find themselves penniless and ostracised by society. When a relative contrives to put an '*eligible parti*' under an obligation to make Amelia an offer, Amelia has to decide whether or not to stand by her principles . . . and face the consequences of turning down what might be her only chance to escape her unbearable situation.